MW01620908

THE MEMOIRS OF JONBENET BY KATHY ACKER

MICHAEL DU PLESSIS

TRENCHART: SURPLUS

∮

LES FIGUES PRESS
Los Angeles

The Memoirs of JonBenet by Kathy Acker
FIRST EDITION

Text design by Teresa Carmody

ISBN 13: 978-1-934254-36-3
ISBN 10: 1-934254-36-3
Library of Congress Control Number: 2012942153

Les Figues Press thanks its subscribers for their support and readership. Les Figues Press is a 501c3 organization. Donations are tax-deductible.

Les Figues would like to acknowledge the following individuals for their generosity: Peter Binkow, Johanna Blakley, Lauren Bon, Chris and Diane Calkins, Pam Ore, Coco Owen.

Les Figues Press titles are available through:
Les Figues Press, <http://www.lesfigues.com>
Small Press Distribution, <http://www.spdbooks.org>

Copy editing and production assistance: David Emanuel, Militza Jean-Felix, Erin Kilduff, and Emma Williams.

TrenchArt 7/4

Book 5 of 6 in the TrenchArt Surplus Series.

This project is supported in part by a generous grant from the National Endowment for the Arts.

Post Office Box 7736
Los Angeles, CA 90007
United States
www.lesfigues.com

For everyone who's died in Colorado.

(It's never too late to write teen poetry.)

CONTENTS

INTRODUCTION

BY PEGGY KAMUF

"I don't know who's writing this," we read early on in these pages (5).

To think about the experience called writing is to realize that such not-knowing-who-writes is the condition of its happening at all. The responsibility of a signatory is, for all intents and purposes, nothing but the legal fiction required by conventions of copyright. It is finally superfluous to what happens whenever writing takes a literary turn. For this turn has necessarily to pass through the device, figure, or projection of some other who is not the writer. Which is why one can identify the minimal condition of fiction with "the altogether bare device of being-two-to-speak."[1]

In *The Memoirs of JonBenet by Kathy Acker,* this device is not merely laid bare; it is hyperbolized and taken through a dizzyingly inventive whirl of additional turns. The more one reads, the less sense it makes to ask the question "who's writing this?" Writers here channel other writers the way dolls have dolls of their own. No sooner does the dead writer Kathy Acker come back to animate the doll JonBenet than JonBenet the doll procures a Kathy Acker™ doll. Or else K.A. transforms into H.P. Lovecraft or William Burroughs, while identifying with O of the *Story of O.* Du Plessis's is the art of a ventriloquist so

---

Jacques Derrida, *Given Time: I. Counterfeit Money,* trans. Peggy Kamuf (London: University of Chicago Press, 1992), 153.

artful he can carry many voices inside other voices. It is artful as well in the sense of being full to the brim with quotations, allusions, and references. Literature, music, painting, film course through the veins of the text. A large library is mobilized, of multiple languages, genres, and periods. And this artfulness in turn underscores the insistence here on artifice as antidote to the fakery and pretense of nature. The natural pretense is everywhere, but its headquarters, according to the one (or the several ones) writing these memoirs, is Boulder, Colorado, whose very name proclaims the artlessness of sheer rock.

It is the utter incongruity of Kathy Acker returning all the way from the dead only to end up in Boulder that gives the initial impetus to *Memoirs* and sustains a caustic overtone throughout. Not since Baudelaire's *Poor Belgium*, perhaps, has any place on earth been so vilified or humiliated. But whereas Baudelaire aims to wound fatally with the assault of his mean-spirited spite, du Plessis unsettles everything with an irony so multifaceted and multivoiced that its blows land only to veer off in another direction.

This turning aside of pointed critique may, however, simply confirm the snowglobe effect, which Kathy Acker denounces in the first lines of *Memoirs*: "Boulder is an ugly snowglobe that someone bought in a cheap airport gift store and stuck at the foot of the Rocky Mountains" (3). Although Acker complains that she is trapped inside Boulder's snowglobe, one senses all the same that the challenge posed to the writing of *Memoirs* is how to penetrate this hard, boulder-like, hermetically-sealed globe from somewhere that is outside without being simply without, somewhere else that is all the same withheld within.

It is not a matter of shattering the illusion of simulation so as to emerge into the real or true world; this is not yet another updating of the allegory of the cave, à la *The Matrix* or *The Truman Show*. And it is not a matter either of the decadent aesthetic of a Des Esseintes (who is mentioned in passing) fleeing the natural light of day. For if there are only simulations, including and most insidiously the simulation of non-simulation called "nature," then this very notion is ruined and one is left somewhere beyond the coordinates of a representable, simulatable world. Rather than a world "out there" (outside the snowglobe, as it were) that can be reliably pointed to, *Memoirs* knows a world in which dolls are as real as the children who are as fake as dolls. Death is here the only index of reality, which is why the "dead doll child" JonBenet is warned against "dying to be real": "You must never, ever, die to be real. It's disgusting," intone in unison the three painted portraits of the Synnot children hanging in the Denver Art Museum (65).

Sin not, children.

Dying to be real is the suicidal temptation for dolls like JonBenet: "I warn you!" says the Kathy Acker™ doll when her voice string is pulled, "they install Reality not merely as crude necessity, as enforced limit, but as object of aspirations and wishes! Can you imagine?" (10-11). Such a Reality Principle (her words) is, then, for the dead dolls of this world, the path taken by their death drive. But did Freud in fact say anything else? Freud, who also knew a thing or two about uncanny dolls that one could wish into living reality? Reality Principle, Pleasure Principle, or Death Drive: what's the difference finally when the PP and DD are always detouring through each other while trying to reach their goals even as both are forced to submit to the third, to the dreaded Reality Principle?[2] Can *Memoirs* rewrite this scenario through repeated warnings against the Reality Principle? In other words, will not JonBenet have to die despite being already "a dead doll child"?

2. See Sigmund Freud, *Beyond the Pleasure Principle,* passim.

The trinity of the Sin Not children think they can tell the difference between two deaths, a death in fiction and a death in reality: "Dear JonBenet, we don't know how to tell you this. There are two deaths. Everything's doubled, haven't you noticed? You must see. One death is fiction—that's the good death. The other is real death, dying to be real" (65). Having been warned, once again, JonBenet is then dragged by "Ms. Realism" onto the bus for the ride back to Boulder. Will she heed the warning? Will she try not to die the real death? Yes, of course. The chapter ends: "I am JonBenet. These are my memoirs. I don't want to be real, never ever" (66).

But wishing doesn't make it so. Or rather, given the ineluctable detours of the *Lustprinzip* through the Reality Principle, death finds a way to make even the most unreal doll real, which is to say, dead. Boulder, that most unreal of places, makes real. It is the unreal Reality Principle, as Kathy Acker (unless it's Kathy Acker™) shouts to the university audience that eagerly gathers to hear her lecture: "I must warn you that JonBenet will be murdered again, sacrificed to the Reality Principle that is Boulder. Or rather murdered for the Boulder effect: the Unreal that maintains steadfastly, arrogantly, unstoppably, that it is Real" (74).

The scene of this haranguing lecture, which is titled with a nod to Nietzsche "Why Stephen King Writes Such Bad Novels," could feed the reader's speculation about one of the impulses channeling the terrific energy of *Memoirs*. Whoever has done time in the university under the charge of professing literature can no doubt recognize the urge to unleash a similar broadside attack on illusions cherished among a public of students force-fed their idea of "literature" by the best-seller industry. This scene is at once the most plausible and the least likely, the least dreamlike and the most outrageous of *Memoirs*. It stabs brutally close to the core of beliefs sustaining the unreal reality, the real unreality of "Boulder"—a place name that becomes dislodged metonymically from culturally colorless Colorado and starts to roll through the roster of the fifty states, flattening everything in its path, until the cops move in to halt the lecture and haul Kathy Acker (or her replica doll) off the stage.

One may suspect, however, that the exhilarating hilarity of such scenes is itself working to counter and divert the somber realization that a possible future has been closed down, like a murdered child. Through the extravagant expenditure of its accumulated riches, *Memoirs* performs a kind of literary potlatch as if there were no tomorrow. But unlike a Trobriand Island clan chief, du Plessis cannot see or know that there is a recipient of all this gift-giving. And in that, he is like every true writer, burning up the very certainty that these gifts are his to give. "I don't know who's writing this," he writes, leaving to others the chance to read and receive it as they may. It is a chance that you can now look forward to.

Peggy Kamuf
Los Angeles, CA, 2011

THE MEMOIRS OF JONBENET

BY KATHY ACKER

Chapter One: How I Became JonBenet by Kathy Acker

Boulder is an ugly snowglobe that someone bought in a cheap airport gift store and stuck at the foot of the Rocky Mountains. Boulder is the snowglobe in which I've been trapped for eight years. Somewhere between the Island of Misfit Toys and the Valley of the Dolls lies my maximum-security snowglobe. The air is thinner here than Jacqueline Susann ever imagined, and the silence lasts forever. I'm drowning in a vacuum, surrounded on all sides by the yards of gravel and bark that my neighbors consider landscaping.

The silence is a threat, ready at any minute to tear into shrieks, gunfire, explosions. But it never does. Therein lies its power—the threat that is silence in small-town America, smugly silent like a rapist in a stocking mask. This silence is more than just that of menacing individuals, it is the sound of institutions quietly, efficiently, unstoppably at work, altering DNA codes, slipping radioactive waste into the landscape, readying weapons for new wars. The very trees that line the—silent—strips of sidewalk have the swagger of this silence. Every night at 10:30 sharp the citizens of Boulder emerge from their cozy quiet cottages with the Siberian husky-Labrador-coyote-Chow-German shepherd mix that every home in Boulder has as a totemic animal, straining at its leash, ready to take a shit before retiring for the night. And the same game plays itself out every morning, again, at 7:30 exactly.

How they smile, the citizens of Boulder, nodding quietly, little dreaming of the strange and terrifying metamorphosis that has occurred in their midst, miraculous as nuclear power, violent as genetic engineering. You see, Boulder is the place where I've turned into JonBenet, a grown-up doll who looks in the mirror, sees nothing there, and likes it like that. How did this happen? An accident of radioactive waste, a side effect of tampering with gene codes? A mistake of military technology, wafted on the wind from Colorado Springs?

But my transformation is unremarkable here. Can a snowglobe contain the whole world, hold all the threat of the universe? Boulder stays a toytown, a snow village even in full summer.

Nothing happens under the thick Plexiglas Colorado sky that domes this snowglobe in which I've become JonBenet. It's midday, and very warm, and I'm in a Boulder bathroom, with dingy floral linoleum and no windows. Bathrooms never have windows in Boulder. But they do have mirrors, solid as the ones in mental hospitals, except that this mirror doesn't show me anything of my perfect face. It's afternoon in Boulder. It's summer. Everyone's happy and silent except me, for I listen, heart pounding, for shrieks, gunfire, explosions.

I'm not really JonBenet. I'm a plastic doll that looks exactly like her, her double, precise in every detail.

I'm not really a JonBenet doll. I would have told you the truth sooner, but I didn't think you would believe me, and I wanted to get your attention and win your confidence. You see, I'm really Kathy Acker, a dead woman writer come back to life in this village of the damned. I'm a bigger, better O now than I ever was. Kathy-O. When O was a young girl, alive then, above all, she wanted a man to take care of her. In her dream, the town was the repository of all dreams. A town that was always decaying. In the center of this town her father had hanged himself. This can't be true, Kathy-O thought, because I've never had a father. In her dream, she searched for her father.

No, let me tell you the real truth. Bear with me. Anything can happen in Boulder.

I'm a dead writer trapped in the body of a plastic doll.

I'm a plastic doll trapped in the body of a dead writer.

Both of us are trapped in a snowglobe.

I don't know who's writing this, Kathy or JonBenet.

Chapter Two: Kathy Acker™ Speaks

Adorable, unpredictable moppet that I am, I've just snuck out of my impressively secure Tudor house, and I'm off to the Toys-R-Us store on 28th Street. In blue gingham and curls, adorability makes me invincible; moppethood puts a force field all around me. Like a Shirley Temple assassin, like a Killer Kewpie, I take those whimsical bus lines—the Hop, the Skip, the Jump—all on my own, like any adult, paying a quarter that seems awfully big in my childish fingers each ride. Today I'm JonBenet, Kewpie, and Shirley Temple doll in one and the same toy body.

I'm not allowed to be out on my own, not really.

But today is special, better than a birthday, or a pageant, or Christmas.

Today is the day the Kathy Acker™ doll gets released.

"Where are you off to?" ask the grown-ups, the drivers, the ladies, the techno-hippies, on the buses. I bat my eyelashes and giggle. It always makes them shut up: giggles and eyelashes—the best weapons in a doll child's arsenal.

Still, once I get to Toys-R-Us, I can't help but be struck by how little the toyshop resembles the magical emporium of models and make-believe that one would expect from fairytales. This is no enchanted carrousel, with garlanded griffins, lolling-tongued unicorns, gilded geldings, ingratiating tame dragons ready to fly anywhere out of Boulder. At least

Toys-R-Us is a bit less Puritan than the Play Fair Toys across 28th. Less Puritan perhaps, but the Toys-R-Us on 28th still looks like a supermarket in some stark regime of totalitarian capitalism. Like Boulder itself, I guess. The Toys-R-Us store could be a dead ringer for a penitentiary, one of those Big Houses for which Colorado is famous, only this time, it's a Big House for Little People. Everyone's a prisoner here, even the toys. It's a necropolis for stillborn childhoods, I muse, briefly sidetracked by my reveries, tilting my head in a manner calculated to melt hard hearts.

But I've a mission to accomplish. Security's tough—metal detectors and alarms loom to discourage theft, dour and muscle-bound uniformed store guards wait to deal with shameless or desperate shoplifters who aren't awed by alarms and metal detectors. Boulder believes in private property. And it's fiercely private about its property, like Little Lord Fauntleroy is about his emotions and his sex life. Soon, dear reader, all too soon, I shall encounter that ill-fated boy doll.

Enough, though, of memories and anticipations—today's a red letter day. Today is the day I get to buy the Kathy Acker™ doll that has just come onto the toy market. I've been saving for weeks, in secret. Kathy Acker™ will be just my secret, my very own.

She stands a full 12 inches tall, with tiny tattoos and tinier piercings. She's as buff as Lara Croft but a much better role model for little girls—or boys—who are interested in the arts as an action-adventure career. She's a talking doll, thanks to a voice box and a cord in the back of her neck. Her legs stand firmly, challengingly, apart, her arms rest akimbo, her face set in a doll-mask to confront impersonality. She's a speaking likeness of Kathy Acker™, the original. I've dreamt of Kathy Acker™ so often that I know I'll recognize her anywhere, especially here in Toys-R-Us on 28th Street, in doll-form, the doll dream of a doll child.

She has that trademark buzz cut, the one long dangly earring, even tiny bits of finger armor on each hand. And she comes with four costume changes—

Kathy as O, plus corset, chains, and telltale ring with name-tag disk under her skirt, Kathy in full-body fetish armor as Don Quixote the sexual warrior, Kathy as Pip, in a floppy velvet Victorian-gothic number, then, Kathy in swaggering corsair's boots and hat, all twelve inches the swashbuckler, plus an eye patch with skull and crossbones, as Pussy King of Pirates, complemented by a miniature parrot. She retails for $24.95. Each of the outfits and sets of accessories sells for $14.95.

Were Kathy never to be removed from her box, she'd be bound to be a collector's item—a challenge from the art world to the corporate greed of generic toy makers inundating us with their Barbies, their Skippers, their Furbies, their Bratz. She's at least as good as an Ozzy Osbourne figure. I worry that my grown-ups would complain if I bring one of those miniature metalheads home. But what am I saying? My grown-ups can't tell the difference between metalhead and World Wrestling Foundation dolls. Stupid as they are, they don't expect Kathy and me to have a pact, a secret mission.

Or perhaps a Jim Morrison Lizard King adventure doll? No, I'm just distracted by totalitarian capitalism in the Toys-R-Us store on 28th Street. It's Kathy Acker™ or nothing. I've dreamt of this moment for weeks. Kathy's an art doll, ideal for a doll girl like me. I don't think I ever could never-remove-her-from-her-box. When I get through the towering rows of metal shelving, tilting bullyingly inwards as I look upwards, like perspectives in *The Toyshop of Dr. Caligari*, to the aisle with the Kathy Acker™ display—not at all as spectacular as I'd expected but at least that keeps attention away from me— it's love at first sight. She's my new favorite toy and I want to hug her to my chest forever, she's that cute with her buzz cut, her finger armor, her little tattoos, and that single earring.

I gather her up with the four outfits and accessory cases in my plump childish arms and rush to the checkout. I pay the money in dollar bills, quarters, and even smaller change (sure signs of broken piggy banks back home, of weeks of excited and secretive saving). All of this is so wonderfully, enchantingly cute that even the stony-faced prison-guard employees are won over. No one can resist my charms, and no one notices what doll I'm buying, so I'm spared any comments.

Then it's on the Jump, the Skip, the Hop in reverse order, with the same bus drivers, ladies, and techno-hippies. The overhanging trees dangle branches like stranglers' arms, while the junipers brace themselves to jostle you off the sidewalk like thugs with a bone to pick. I hug the Kathy Acker™ doll to my chest and whisper through the cardboard and plastic, "I love you, Kathy Acker™." Reader, if I could just make you see... but no, the scene is far too dear for words.

I arrive at my cozy, secure, impressive Tudor.

I'm home, home with Kathy Acker™.

I unlock the front door and rush up the stairs to my doll-child's bedroom, where, once I've shut the door, I collapse in a sprawl of Toys-R-Us bags.

Alone, alone with Kathy Acker™.

My clever, urgent little fingers quickly open the boxes. Kathy Acker™ stands in the center of my room dressed in her Don Quixote the sexual warrior outfit.

I reach behind her neck and pull the cord of her voice box.

"WHY SHOULD I EVEN PARODY MYSELF?" the doll shrieks. "IT'S YOUR WORLD THAT IS A PARODY NOT I!"

Wow. This is going to be better than I thought. But first, some volume adjustment.

I find the volume dial at the back of her neck. I turn it down and hope that no one in our house heard the outburst. That's better. We are all very polite in this Tudor house.

"I am a makeshift memorial to identity, on the pavement, at the intersection, Mylar balloons, plastic flowers, votive candles, and hideous teddy bears wrapped in barbed wire, where the drive-by, the bombing, the family murder, the shoot-out, the fatal car crash took place. O, not X, marks the spot where identity became a victim."

She intones, "I am all doll parts. As all female rebels have been. Ask Courtney Love.

"What is identity if not prosthesis? What is selfhood if not toy parts? Where is the Empire of Selfsameness if not in its props, in a series of proppings, in prosthesis again? And what better model for the prosthetic props of the self than the dead doll child, JonBenet, Mary Rose, Wendy, the Little Match Girl, the Little Mermaid, Pinocchio, Little Nell, Baby Jesus?"

Does she always talk like this?

"Talking is stealing. All language belongs to the fathers, the grown-ups, words are their private property. Therefore, all true speech must be PLAGIARISM!

"PLAGIARISM—THE ONLY WAY WE CAN SET WORDS FREE! THE SELF—IT'S ONLY A PROP! *ALL SELVES ARE DOLLS, DEAD DOLLS!*"

I adjust the volume dial again.

"Never believe their reality.

"Never believe their lies.

"All words are lies.

"All reality is a lie.

"Therefore, what is not real must be better than their lie of reality.

"Never believe in what is real.

"Never, most of all, believe that what is real is better, JonBenet."

I'm just glad that I didn't play with her voice box in Toys-R-Us, otherwise we'd both now be in Big Trouble for Little People.

"But the enemy of freely stolen words, of doll parts, mixed and matched at will on a black market of our choice, exists! I warn you! She seems a servant of the grown-ups, but she does much more than serve their social order. For she is the one who makes us all believe in and desire the Real! Ah, wherever she goes, the Velveteen Rabbit and other deplorable flunkeys of the Reality Principle follow. And they install Reality not merely as crude necessity, as enforced limit, but as object of aspirations and wishes! Can you imagine? It is she who makes the Little Mermaid dream of human legs and a real prince, she who makes the Velveteen Rabbit happy to be discarded and burnt, she who makes Pinocchio want to be a real boy. She is the foe of all dolls, toys, cyborgs, replicants, robots, androids, humanoids, androgynes, ghosts, and other creatures of moonlight and half-light.

"Beware her more than anything else! Never trust her ruses and her emissaries, who take as many forms as dreams but always give themselves away by their dullness. She is a Traitor to the Feminine and a Collaborator with the Masculine. She is the Death Mother who delivers you over to the Absent Father. She has sold toy magic for stale authenticity. She is the very spirit of Boulder. She makes Stephen King write such bad novels! She is your nemesis, JonBenet!"

How does she know my name? Is there some special imprinting program included for only \$24.95? This is mystifying. Who could Kathy Acker™ be warning me against?

Still, Kathy Acker™ is the best doll, the best friend a girl doll like me could ever have. Only which one of us is really the doll?

I don't have much time to ponder this conundrum, because I hear a creak that's trying too hard to be unobtrusive downstairs. I hear a clatter. There's a series of muffled thumps. Then something—or someone—comes up the stairs.

Quiet and quick, clever mousy, clever birdy that I am, I pop the doll into her box, shove the outfit and accessory cases in with her, and push all of this to the back of my closet.

Another clatter.

Another creak.

The door to my room begins to open,

soundlessly, very slowly, as if in a nightmare, as if underwater.

Perhaps I'm thinking *underwater* because of the cruel watery blue light that gleams under the door and around its edges, a light that becomes ever sharper as the door continues to open silently.

Now the door is open.

And someone—or something—is coming in.

Chapter Three: O in CO

"Last night again, I dreamed that I was dead," O thinks, "or am I dead and dreaming now? I dreamt that I was Kathy Acker, the dead woman writer. It was a dream of insufferable, insupportable sadness," O realizes, "this dream in which I'm not a character, but an author, a dead one, one who imagines herself to be a doll."

The end of O's story gives us two possibilities: first, she chooses death because Sir Stephen is about to leave her; second, she goes back to Roissy, where Sir Stephen abandons her. But O never seems to have much of a choice. From the get-go, she seems ready to be ditched. What if she ends up abandoned, left, forgotten even, by both Sir Stephen and René, O's first lover, the one who got her into all of this? O went back to Roissy all right, which beneath its gothic paraphernalia and sex shop décor turned out to be as humdrum as an American suburb. In fact, Roissy is an American suburb. More accurately, it's a small town—albeit with a big suburban feel—in America. It's in Boulder, Colorado that O ends up, seduced, abandoned, and, most cruelly of all (ah, nothing smarts like the pain of unintended cruelty), forgotten.

Those famous decadent chrysanthemums the color of sulfur faded quickly from the blank screen of O's mind as dusty juniper bushes sprang up in their place, bristling like briar roses in a fairytale, with only yards of bark and gravel for variation. But the air, thin at this altitude, so unbreathable that she could only wheeze unbecomingly, always serves to remind O that she is not in a fairytale. She feels trapped, prey to the pangs of claustrophobia, which is altogether different from the imprisonment and bondage she's welcomed before. Forgotten by both René and Sir Stephen, O turns into a ghost trapped in an eternal summer sublease.

Growing older, O herself forgets why she's in Boulder, Colorado. She notices the O at the end of the state name. Here, in the embrace of the full circle itself embraced by its semi-circle, two moons, one full and one half, two absences, one a whole emptiness, the other incomplete, O feels herself uncomfortable. Why is she in Boulder, CO? O can't but notice that her letter appears in the names of both the town and the state. Is there some mystical significance in this conjunction, this insistence of letters? A fate determined by the alphabet? If there is, she can't decipher it.

Mostly, O's thoughts circle around—she is O, remember—all the way back through Sir Stephen, the daddy, the killer, to René, the daddy's boy, the true abandoner, whom sometimes in her furious blankness, in the airless atmosphere, O thinks of (with bitterness, with regret) as Little Lord Fauntleroy. Here is what O thinks, as she stares out of her window in a sublease in Boulder, Colorado, to see a vista of storage spaces like rows of outhouses, a tarred courtyard, trucks and SUV's and 4x4's all with the same meaningless bumper stickers, a meandering of grass slantwise through summertime cracks in the tar, the tilted and battered grills on which her new neighbors, hippies who work 9 to 5 in the software industry, grill veggie burgers and tofu dogs in a haze of lighter fluid that makes O's eyes smart and burn, as they used to, so long ago, before she was ditched and then erased, here in Boulder, Colorado, when René and then Sir Stephen whipped her and then said they loved her, when she was in Roissy before

Roissy became Boulder. Once, O noticed that the hippie couple keep cages in their living room above her apartment. She was excited and nostalgic before she realized that the hippie couple keep large birds and the totemic Boulder Siberian husky-Labrador-coyote-Chow-German shepherd in those cages. She's never spoken to the neighbors since.

O thinks incessantly about René:

> Absence is the motif in all my writing and all my thinking about you. "You," second-person singular, source of lyricism, invention, and lust, perhaps because of your absence. Absences of all sorts—who would have thought absence to be so malleable, so protean? Physical distance, time not spent together, apartness, aloofness, sleep, out-of-it-ness, drunkenness, gone-ness, preoccupation, the absence of the always premature departure. How male. My father, absent always, already dearly departed, dead two years before his death, dead a long time before the disease was done with eating his body.

O thinks circularly about René:

> I'm bored. I'm anxious. I feel like I'm constantly taking a series of emotional GRE's, and I'm never told what my score is.
>
> I'm afraid we're inventing something that isn't there.
>
> Why is sex with you another blank?
>
> Waiting, as you consider it, is fine but there comes a moment when the conditions you impose outweigh any present emotions. "I can't be with you until..." translates into "I can't be with you until caution becomes indifference." Yes, as you say over and over again, you've made me feel again; truly, I do feel again, enough to be able to tell that I'm only telling myself that I feel with you.
>
> You, always absent, never wholly there.

> I read your writing in your absence and it's clear and limpid, but I also see how absent you are from this writing.
>
> Absence isn't impersonality. Impersonality is a chosen quality; absence—redundancy! double O!—is a lack.
>
> You do almost anything except be with me. Anyone who can prefer to look at the Boulder Creek rather than be with a lover is not a lover. One cannot possibly know anything about nature or beauty or truth when the Boulder Creek appears worth contemplating.

If O seems galled, that is because the last is a particularly nettling recollection.

O thinks about René because René is not, has never been, there:

> "Be true to thyself," you say, lost in a truism, absent in the commonplace, an absence bestowed by glibness. It's a long time together; it's no time at all. Absence produces my sense of the test, perhaps because I have to project to fill this void. Better to be tested invisibly all the time than for all our time together to add up to nothing at all. You say you are fiercely independent. Deeply private. Ferociously private. I wake up at two a.m. with the utter clarity that I've invented something, and that I've played games with you, with myself, to dissimulate that. Absence of stories, rituals, reassurances. Absence of accumulation. You say you don't say you're in love, you act in love, but that's an alibi for doing neither. I face the stunning double negative of your absence.

O rereads what Kathy Acker has written about her, O. "When O was a young girl, alive then, above all, she wanted a man to take care of her. In her dream, the town was the repository of all dreams. A town that was always decaying. In the center of this town her father had hanged himself. In her dream, she searched for her father."

Is she searching? Is she questing? Isn't her quest always the circle, self-completion? Her sigil is the ouroboros, round like the metal name tag she still wears from the ring in her labia. O decides to write René a letter, but first she wants to look up the letter O in the dictionary. They're playing my letter, O laughs.

What? You thought O had no sense of humor? How else could she have put up, not with the tortures (those were tolerable), but with those insufferably pompous men? She's worn her name like a mask, her mask-like name, to have the last laugh at those asinine, humorless men. O can only laugh, helplessly. And now Kathy Acker joins the ranks of those who write on her. When will they hear my voice, wonders O, beyond the trellised bars, the confining devices, of free indirect speech? *Discours indirect libre*, another joke! Free *and* indirect, an oxymoron? She wonders.

And here are some of the words that O reads in the dictionary:

> oaf, oafish, Oahuan, oak, oak apple, oak beauty, oak blight, oak bore, oak brown, oak chestnut, oaken, oakenshaw, oak family... oasis, oasitic, oast, oasthouse, oat... obeah, obeche, obedience, obediencer, obediency, obedient, obediential, obedientiary, obediently, obedient plant, obeisance, obeisant... *Oberschule,* obese, obesity, obex, obey, obeyable, obeyance, obeyer, obfirm, obfusc, obfuscable, obfuscate, obfuscatory... obituary, object, objectable, objectant, object ball, object color, objectee, object glass, objectifiable, objectification, objectify, objection, objectionability, *objet d'art*, objuration, objurgate... obligate, obligation... oblige, obliged... oblique, oblique angle, oblique case, oblique coordinate, oblique drawing, oblique fault... obliquity, obliterable, obliterate,

obliteratingly, obliteration, obliterative, obliviate, oblivion, oblivionize, oblivious, obliviously, obliviousness, oblivescence, oblocutor, oblong, oblongate, obloquious, obloquy, obtumesce... obscene, obscure... obsess, obsession... obsolete, obsolescence, obverse... odd, oddball, odd-eyed, odd fish, oddish, oddity, odium, off, off and on, off-bar, off-beat, off-center, off-color, offhand... old school, old world, oleander, olfactory, om, *omnium gatherum*, omnivore, oneiric, oneirocritics, one-lung, one-man, oneself, onyx, opal, opaline, open, open-ended, operate, ophryon... ordeal, ordeal bean, ordeal tree, orient, oriental, oscillate... ostensible, ostensible partner, ouroboros, out, outscout, oval, ovarian, ovary, over, overlook, overly, overripe, oxymoron, oyster fork, ozone, ozostomia, ozotype.
Over.

What beads are missing from O's rosary of O's? The words tell O nothing. Sir Stephen was not a father complex but a daddy fix. And René, daddy's boy, his mother's son? She loved René. She has waited for him to call her, here, in Roissy, in Boulder, in Colorado. She told him not to call, the only time she has issued a command. "I hear and I obey," O recalls bitterly, with a wry smile. O has a mordant wit. O has a soft heart. O has a liquid center. O is no blank slate, no blank stare.

"Dear René," she writes. She crosses out the name, except for the initial. "Dear R," it reads. She crosses out "Dear," so that it reads, simply, "R." The anonymity of the alphabet works best in epistolary fiction and all epistolary fiction is about absence, like all letters, alphabetical or no.

O's letter:

R,

It rained all day on the day that you never phoned. If you told me that you'd call and I told you not to call, and then you didn't call, on the day you never phoned, does that mean that you actually didn't call? Did you not call in the sense that you decided and chose not to call or were you just doing what I'd asked you? Did you make up your own mind not to call me or did you not call because I said I didn't want you to call? It rained all day and when I walked down a hill, a bearded man with two Rottweilers straining like hellhounds at their leashes asked me where the nearest McDonald's was. I suppose there must be a McDonald's in Boulder, yes, even in Boulder, where anything can happen, but I don't know where it is. I don't know where anything is in Boulder. I still get lost trying to find the apartment that I'm subleasing. Everything looks like everything else to me in Boulder. There are no landmarks. I may as well be walking in place in a diorama that is spooling past, repeating itself every so often. It's calming and unnerving.

You never phoned on the day it rained all day. This wasn't the first time you didn't phone when you said you would but this was the first time you didn't phone when I'd asked you not to phone. Every time you hadn't phoned before, I'd asked you, noncommittally, nonchalantly, pressingly, desperately, to call. The day it rained all day, the day you never phoned, was the first time that I'd asked you not to phone. So I don't know if your never calling means that you did what I asked or that you decided on your own, against my unexpressed but so transparent wishes, not to phone, never to phone again. From now on there can just be this long angry silence between us. It's the silence of your never phoning on the day it rained all day, the day you were meant to phone, the day I asked you not to phone. This silence started on the day you never phoned, the day it rained all day in the silence of your never phoning again.

She rereads the letter.
She decides not to send it.
She signs it, nevertheless:

XXOXX
O

Chapter Four: The Carpet Out of Time

Today Kathy Acker isn't feeling herself. Dead woman writer, she stares into the solid, unbreakable plastic mirror in the bathroom without windows. Because she sees nothing in her mirror, she touches her face and marvels at its transformation into smooth, lifelike, unlined plastic. Today is a day for change, she decides. She's been thinking too much about O, O who will give up everything for a man. Pathetic. Perhaps it's time for a change of gender, thinks the dead woman writer. But why does Kathy Acker nonetheless feel as though she were on the verge of an anxiety attack? She glances into the corridor outside her Boulder sublease bathroom. It's that silence again. She looks down, and notices the verge of the carpet just outside the door, lurking like the panic attack she's verging on.

"If only I could capture the unmitigated horror of life in Boulder," wishes Kathy Acker, "I might be able to ward off my panic attack."

Boulder: where eugenics couples with software to secure the perfect reproduction of middle-class bodies, bodies that desire only perfect reproduction.

Boulder: where white-collar heaven beckons under pitiless white-collar skies.

Boulder: where cotton-ball, cotton-candy cirri hang over the Flatirons, like the prettiest, freshest mushroom clouds ever.

Boulder: where the Pied Piper lured the children of Hamelin and where they grow old but never grow up. Where Never-Never Land was colonized by the U. S. of A.

Boulder: where lumbering adults play hacky sack, tag, beanbag, frisbee, volleyball, all day long. Forever.

Boulder: where lunatic snow angels attack.

Boulder: where white men eternally celebrate the 4th of July, bare chests, sweat, minor explosions, beer.

Boulder: where a city ordinance makes it illegal to have upholstered furniture out of doors. With its soft spot for pyromania, Boulder can't resist the temptation of flammable outdoor targets. Boulder burns so readily that it invites arson.

Boulder: where the mountains shove up against the town, closing in like walls in an Edgar Allan Poe story.

And this leads Kathy Acker inevitably to the even more unmitigated horror of domestic space in Boulder. "Perhaps if I could describe at least that, I would be able to ward off my panic attack, pressing in like the mountains, like the sky.

"All Boulder apartments are exactly the same," Kathy Acker declaims, eyes shut. "Structures of the 1970s, they promised the good life of the American Bicentennial in the raw materials—particle board, polyresin, reinforced tupperware, drywall, polyester, pressed wood shingle, polyurethane—the flammable and cheap fabric from which the American Dream is spun. All apartments are alike: beige carpeting, gray from years of snow stains, pet stains, brown kitchen sticky from years of unsavory vegetarian grease, dank bathroom in dark green. Look, the A-frame with its two-story wood-burning fireplace—cozy, no? A wood-burning stove in every A-frame, those kitchens in once-modish browns, those bathrooms of an avocado color trendy long ago: hippie dreams met money in a studio jam session bliss-out, in a free love encounter of leisure architecture and rising real estate values. Olive green, brown, beige, camouflage colors still, after Vietnam, violently neutral, U. S. foreign policy turned domestic design. Outside, below the junipers, yards of gravel and bark. Do you know that the local gay bar was called the Yard of Ale? Boulder, the Yard of Yards, domestic interior as exteriority, space as its own measurement, for its own empty sake.

"All are filthy now, not with the heroic filth of poverty or despair, but with the dirt of middle-class transience, the shifting attentions, the final shiftiness of the populations who have passed through Boulder, insubstantial as wireless technology, with a residue like nuclear waste.

"All are alike, beneath the filth, built to a scale that contests bodies, human or doll—as though Boulder were a dingy other planet, its apartments constructed according to a geometry that renders them uninhabitable by humanoids. Khaki, tie-dye, lighter fluid igniting a thousand barbecues for charred tofu dogs. Mattings and clumpings of pet hair, clumpings and mattings of juniper, juniper like shapeless hands at the windows, at the doors, like an offshoot, an outgrowth of the carpet.

"Everywhere in Boulder, the creeping, omnipresent, utterly inescapable fungus of the beige wall-to-wall carpet, once bright beige at least, but now a sullen gray, like an overcast sky, the kind of sky one never sees in Boulder, where the sun shines 360 days a year. Perhaps this carpet is the revenge of the weather, a meteorological curse, Boulder's bad weather underfoot if not overhead? Can a village be strangled by the crawling, all-consuming, wall-to-wall, door-to-door, street-to-street, suburb-to-suburb beige carpet? Even on the hottest summer day the carpet recalls the filthy snow that blankets us for nine months of the year. If triffids were carpet, they'd be this dingily colorless nylon bodysnatcher.

"Oh, winter warmed us all right, mixing memory with desire with a lot of other, less easy-to-name things in our carpets. Summer surprised us, as we stared at our carpets. Surely it must have expanded this past season? What lies buried beneath the grayish beige of wall-to-wall carpet in Boulder? The corpse under the underpile, that strange lump the vacuum cleaner always bumps against? Unreal suburb: Boulder, Louisville, Superior, Broomfield, Lafayette, Gunbarrel, Highlands Ranch: unreal. Has it begun to sprout, the corpse you buried beneath your beige wall-to-wall carpet last year?

"All apartments in Boulder are the same because only happiness tells a new story, because all unhappy families are unhappy in exactly the same way. It's all in the carpet, you see."

Today is a day for change, decides Kathy Acker, dead woman writer. No, not Don Quixote, not Pip, not Pussy King of Pirates. No, she decides, as she stands in the mildewy bathroom with no windows, a different masculinity is needed. She pulls off her finger armor, takes out her long single earring.

"I'll become H.P. Lovecraft, gentleman fictioneer," she laughs. "He knew a thing or two about the colorless colors of small-town America." She strips, and then puts on the clothing slowly, piece by piece, stiff bosom shirt with round cuffs and standing collar, black coat and vest, gray striped trousers, black string tie, and Panama hat.

She is now just under five feet and eleven inches tall, with broad but stooped shoulders, lean to gauntness, with a size fourteen neck that seems too thin to support her large head. She has dark eyes and hair (which is turning a mousy gray—the influence of the carpet, perhaps?) and a long face with an aquiline nose. Her salient feature is a very long chin—a "lantern jaw"—below a small pursed mouth, which gives her a prim look.

She parts her hair on the left and keeps it short, almost in a crew cut. She justifies this coiffure on the grounds that eighteenth-century gentlemen wore their hair thus under their wigs.

Ingrown hairs on her face have bothered her all her life. The only cure for this condition is to grow a beard; but, as a devotee of the clean-shaven Baroque era, Lovecraft-Acker hates all facial hair; she says: "I'd as soon think of wearing a nose-ring as of growing a moustache..."

Her skin is pale from her nocturnal habits. She never likes to tan, and a trace of color in her cheeks seems somehow to be the source of annoyance. Curse the Colorado sun!

She has long, pale, slender hands and feet. Her hands are colder than people expect. "Shaking hands with me is like shaking hands with a corpse," she observes.

In dress, she is clean and neat but ultraconservative in taste. She affects an aggressively old-fashioned appearance, a sedulous cultivation of premature elderliness and sartorial antiquarianism manifesting itself in a stiff bosom shirt, round cuffs, black coat and vest and gray striped trousers, standing collar and black string tie, with austere and reticent manners to match. She dons high-buttoned shoes and carries an old-fashioned change purse. She's used to wearing her father's elegant nineteenth-century garments until they wear out.

Fortunately she has a biography of the gentleman fictioneer at hand, since there is still no image in the mirror, nor will there ever be any image in the mirror. Kathy Acker has to see herself as H.P. Lovecraft in the looking-glass of words alone. "My god, I look like William Burroughs!" she gasps. Might William Burroughs and H.P. Lovecraft fuck at last through the medium of Kathy Acker's sexual transformation? Might there be a cut-up three-way of Acker, Lovecraft, and Burroughs? Consider the possibilities for a truly lurid and prurient fiction! A female-to-male-to-male-on-male clusterfuck! Kathy Acker starts to wonder whether she should write this up and submit it to this year's *Men On Men*. What is their editorial policy? Do they publish work by dead male homoerotic writers channeled by dead woman writers still living in a Boulder sublease? And what if the male homoeroticism occurs all in the same transformed, transforming body... how very trans! But it's beginning to get crowded in here, thinks Kathy Acker of her dead body. Besides, Lovecraft was never, and will never be, a Beat, which is why Kathy Acker has apotropaically called on him against the all-seeing evil eye of the Boulder carpet.

To make her transformation complete by giving her a pronoun reassignment, she utters these words:

"Eldritch, batrachian, tarn, charnel!"

Now beyond and beneath clothes, she's a he. H.P., to be exact. And now he recalls that his mother wished most ardently for a girl, that she had started a hope chest for one. Hence, his mother persistently favored the characteristics of her son that she considered to be feminine. She dressed him in a Little Lord Fauntleroy suit and deliberately tried to feminize him. As a result of his mother's suggestions, the infant Lovecraft for a while insisted, "I'm a little girl."

His approach to sex is so prissy and inhibited that, combined with his high voice and mincing manner, some wonder about his sexual orientation.

"We have sex so strangely these days," whispers H.P. Lovecraft.

He clears his throat, and pronounces in his mincing manner in his high New England voice:

"In relating the circumstances which have led to my confinement within this refuge for the demented that is a sublease in Boulder, I am aware that my present position will create a natural doubt of the authenticity of my narrative. It is an unfortunate fact that the bulk of humanity is too limited in its mental vision to weigh with patience and intelligence those isolated phenomena, seen and felt only by a psychologically sensitive few, which lie outside its common experience."

What will H.P. Lovecraft have to say about the carpet?

"Mayhap the carpet is Cthulhu?" he marvels, then corrects himself.

"'Tis the carpet out of time. 'Tis is an eldritch carpet, verily, as foreseen in the blasphemous secret scrawlings of the Mad Arab, Abdul Alhazred, the most arcane of his writings not even collected in the infamous *Necronomicon*.

"The carpet is like unto a blasted heath, not because of anything that can be seen or heard or handled, but because of something that is imagined. The carpet is not good for imagination, and it does not bring restful dreams at night. It must be this that keeps foreigners away. Upon everything the carpet bestows a haze of restlessness and oppression; a touch of the unreal and grotesque, as if some vital element of perspective or chiaroscuro were awry; the carpet, acres of gray desolation that sprawl open to the ceiling like a great spot eaten by acid."

Lovecraft bends forward at the verge of the carpet to examine it more closely before continuing to speak.

"The carpet is like a fine gray dust or ash which no wind ever seems to blow about, oddly soft. It is only by analogy that one can call the color of the carpet color at all. It is dowered with outside properties and obedient to outside laws. Colors that cannot be put into any words, their shape is monstrous. No sane wholesome colors but the prismatic variants of some diseased underlying tone without a place among the known tints of earth."

Bug-eyed now, he rises, throws his head back, and runs his hands through his crew cut. He messes up the parting.

"The carpet is creeping and creeping and waiting to be seen and heard. What eldritch dream-world is this into which I have blundered?"

Gingerly, unsteadily, he steps out of the bathroom, onto the carpet itself.

"Why is everything so gray and brittle? This carpet is like a glutted swarm of corpse-fed fireflies dancing hellish sarabands over an accursed marsh! The carpet is a nameless intrusion, seething, feeling, lapping, reaching, scintillating, straining, and malignly bubbling in its cosmic and unrecognizable chromaticism; it seems to sweep down in frore gusts from interstellar space."

Sinking to his knees on the carpet itself at last, he proceeds in a hushed, defeated tone, a tone that lacks calm entirely.

"It is just a carpet out of space, out of time—a frightful messenger from unformed realms of infinity beyond all Nature as we know it; from realms whose mere existence stuns the brain and numbs us with the black extra-cosmic gulfs it throws open before our frenzied eyes."

H.P. Lovecraft begins to evaporate, enervated by the carpet.

As he disappears, Kathy Acker shows through him, as though Lovecraft were a fading superimposition.

She speaks now:

"Boulder is the town out of space—no, Boulder is not extraterrestrial, not from beyond the stars, like the Elder Gods. Boulder is simply out of room. It is contracting, claustrophobically, under the pressure of its no-growth laws and under the influx of people who hope against hope that this town will liberate their heartlands. Your Own Private Boulder. Unlucky cosmonauts of inner space, they come to grief inside the confines of Boulder.

"And its carpet."

Kathy Acker stretches herself full-length on the carpet.

It strikes her suddenly how much Lovecraft hated *The Waste Land*. He'd ranted about the "disjointed and incoherent 'poem' called *The Waste Land*" and denounced it as a "practically meaningless collection of phrases, learned allusions, quotations, scraps in general; offered to the public (whether or not as hoax) as something justified by our modern mind with its recent comprehension of its own chaotic triviality and disorganization." Should one apologize to one's cross-gender other self for citing a text which that self hates?

As she ponders, she wonders again about Lovecraft's sexual identity.

She (he) was so sure of herself (himself), she (he) fucked everyone she (he) could get her (his) hands on. There were plenty of them, thinks Kathy Acker about H.P. Lovecraft, regardless of sexual gender. At the same time, because she (he) was sexually ambiguous, she (he) looked sexually innocent. She (He) always said that she (he) wasn't a whore, she (he) never got near sex. She (He) didn't even feel. She (he) might have fucked here and there, now and then, but that didn't matter. In fact, it didn't really happen. Who could be more androgynous?

But from androgyny, she finds herself slipping back, always back, to the subject of men, for it's a small slide from the carpet to the question of men.

As O thinks of men, so Kathy Acker does now.

Circling like O, Kathy Acker thinks from the carpet to men to the carpet.

Did feats of genetic engineering make both men and the carpet? Has something gone awry, as it always does, in these stories?

Men:

> The man bonded with his boychild. He did this on a regular basis.
>
> The man beside me on the bus took the ringing cell phone out of the inside pocket of his jacket, stared at the number of the caller identification, and put the cell phone back in his pocket without answering it. He repeated this a number of times.
>
> The men in the SUV, two in the front, two in the back, all wore insect-eyed sunglasses and baseball caps or sun visors. They were as impersonal as identikit images.
>
> The men jostled me off the sidewalk, not intentionally, for I was entirely irrelevant to their manly lives, but because they needed to occupy a certain set dimension and volume. They had taken off their shirts, a sheen of perspiration on

their torsos, and despite all surface vigor and health, their twenty-year-old trunks appeared oddly artificial, like those of mannequins melting in the heat. Were these men frat boys? Would they set fire to upholstered furniture luckless enough to be out of doors? Were they, themselves, as combustible as they looked?

The man at the traffic light next to me was wearing Lycra shorts, with no shirt, his legs visibly shaven, their smooth extremities in marked contrast to the salt and pepper fuzz erupting all over his torso. There was a sweat stain at his crotch (at any rate I assumed it was sweat) and at the back, above his buttocks. He was pushing a sports bicycle.

I realized he'd just completed the Bolder Boulder marathon. It's what men here like to consider a male rite of passage, like bonding with their sons, like setting fire to couches. Would they one day mistake their sons for couches? I looked around and saw that I was surrounded by hundreds of men, all dressed in Lycra and sweat and cycling gear and body hair (except on their shaved legs), as though I were in a screwball comedy, as though I were on another planet (Planet of Re-Cycling Men), as though I were in a nightmare of repetition, a Hell of Parallel Universes in which only the men remained constant.

When I neared The Fisherman's Angle, on the corner of 19th and Arapahoe, a fishing line and hook swung past me to land in the gutter, over and over. As I got closer, I saw the line and hook were attached to a rod and a man, who, burly, bloody of bloated face, swung the hook and line out again and again into the street and the gutter. He made no effort to stop when I passed, although it was clear that he'd seen me.

The men are either in their twenties and wearing baseball caps over their eyes, concealed anyway by sunglasses, sporting khaki shorts and sandals, with flat, brutal, American feet ready to stomp on the world and any obstacle, or else they are in their forties with a desperate in-shape quality, after their first divorce, before their second, keen to insinuate themselves into some New World Domestic Order. Both types of men dream of reproducing themselves. Their bodies need to take up more space, so the men must keep themselves trim in order to maximize their chances of reproduction.

"I'm glad that my reproduction is mechanical and not sexual," asserts Kathy Acker.

"Straight, gray, male, beige," she intones, amused by the plaintive ay-ay-ay-ay of this internal rhyme.

Then she sinks into the carpet as she might sink into the Boulder Creek. It's been a tiring morning.

As she falls asleep, she hears the voice of H.P. Lovecraft, across time, across space:

"The men are everywhere, like the carpet.
They are beige and threatening like the carpet.
The men are the carpet.
The carpet is the men.
The carpet is everywhere, like the men.
It is beige and threatening like the men.
The carpet sucks up the men.
The man-carpet waits for you."

Chapter Five: Doll Arts

The lecture today at the university, the flagship, the spaceship of Flagstaff Mountain, will be free and open to the public. A philosophy professor and master of decorative arts will speak on the topic of "Doll Arts." Already, the topic alone has drawn a small, Boulder-sized amount of controversy, because the decorator-philosopher holds some idiosyncratic views about the nature of matter. He is staying in the fake-forest green Comfort Inn on Arapahoe with its scab-colored moldings and rank potpourri.

The few intellectuals in the audience think, as they watch the dapper figure, bespectacled and moustached, mount the steps to the stage: "It is this man, with his lofty view of human potentiality, his own strong individual imagery and bold ideas, who has sat down to write the memoirs of a doll, in a style exquisitely suitable, without condescension or bathos, and in a spirit of evident enjoyment. Why?"

He walks up to the podium. He lowers the microphone. He begins to speak in the most measured of voices.

"I was always, among human beings, the only doll with a heart.

"I was always, among human beings, only the doll with a heart.

"I was always the doll with the only heart among human beings."

The audience shifts until they realize that the philosopher-decorator is quoting, so that it takes a while for them to relax enough to commence the usual round of encouraging nods and note-taking.

"We may recall that for the great Georg Wilhelm Friedrich Hegel, the veritable Eagle of Intellect, the history of the world unfolds as Spirit gradually sublates Matter, its antithesis. Once Spirit and Matter become one, the history of the world is done. You may notice that our great Hegel gives the upper hand, the advantage, to Spirit here, for it is Spirit that must conquer Matter to make Matter join Spirit. Thus Spirit initiates and completes the dialectic.

"But what if the dialectic worked the other way around? What if everything worked the other way round?"

There's polite befuddlement, manifested in the hasty rustle of notes and a brief excited susurration. What is he suggesting?

"Ladies and gentlemen," the philosopher-decorator beams benignly, eyes a-twinkle through his spectacles, "I wish to propose that Matter may have the upper hand, that to assume that Spirit alone is capable of agency is wrong-headed, that, in short, the dialectic of the history of the world will be completed when Spirit becomes Matter, not, as Hegel asserted, the other way round.

"Hence, the phenomenon of the talking doll, the perfect inversion of the dialectic that puts Spirit over Matter. The talking doll is speaking matter. Matter speaks, sublates Spirit unto itself, in the body of the talking doll.

"That is why, as we well know, the invert loves the doll, for the doll in fact loves the invert first."

He pauses, before reading, myopically bent, from his minute notes:

> "Have not girls done as much for the doll?—the doll—yes, target of things past and to come? The last doll, the gift given to maturity and old age, is the girl who should have been a boy and the boy who should have been a girl! The love of that last doll was foreshadowed in

> that love of the first. The doll resembles but does not contain life, and the invert or third sex contains life but resembles the doll. The blessed double face! It should be seen only in profile, otherwise it is observed to be the conjunction of the identical cleaved halves of sexless misgiving!"

He looks up, still twinkling. "Ah, but the difference between containing and resembling is so slight, such a mere shade or tint, that we may well believe the doll and the third sex to be Matter over Spirit, Matter containing and resembling, inter-twinedly, undifferentiatedly, Spirit.

"But I am here today for more practical matters," he proceeds, the half-pun concealed in his affably bland manner.

"When I was a little girl I thought that 'decorating' was just something you did to birthday cakes to make them look fancy. Like writing your name and putting flowers and 'Happy Birthday' in delicious pink and blue icing on top of the chocolate frosting.

"I was very surprised to find out that every time my mother had the walls painted or papered, or our furniture got changed around, that was called 'decorating' too.

"That was about a million years ago. Maybe not quite a million, but before they had TV sets anyway, and on rainy days when I couldn't go out and play, I played on the back steps of our house.

"It was on one of those rainy days that I decided those steps would make lovely rooms for my dolls."

The philosopher-decorator has at last arrived at the core of his talk. After a moment's hesitation over his switch in pronoun, the audience is taking notes busily, nodding heads, smiling at each other, and noticing the reference to frequent rainy days as a sign that the philosopher-decorator comes, unmistakably, from somewhere other than Boulder, with its 360 days of sunshine. Perhaps his unusual perceptiveness with regard to dolls may be an effect of weather variations?

"There was pretty carpet on the floor, and yellow wallpaper on the sides, so I really had a head start! Each step became a room, and I found furniture for every room and moved my dolls in. I used to call them 'step-rooms.' There was only one trouble. If anyone wanted to use the back stairs, I had to undecorate them!

"Then one birthday I got a doll house, and I played with it all the time. I never played with my 'step-rooms' again. They languished in that abandon where all forgotten loved objects go—Puff the Magic Dragon, the Velveteen Rabbit, or Winnie-the-Pooh, for example."

He pauses. He would like to say something about JonBenet but fears that it may appear impolite. The thought of abandoned toys disorients him.

"Just as the intersection of two lines on one side of a point suddenly appears again on the other side of the infinite; or the image in a concave mirror, after receding into the infinite, suddenly resurfaces close before us—grace likewise reappears when knowledge has passed through the infinite, so that it appears purest simultaneously in the human body that has either none at all or else infinite consciousness—that is, in the doll or the god, conjunction of the identical cleaved halves of sexless misgiving!

"We should ponder the alchemical hermaphroditism of Spirit and Matter, doll and god. We must contemplate the counter-dialectical inversion of Matter and Spirit. For it is in dolls that Matter speaks, speaking Matter.

"Yes, Matter speaks and Matter dreams. We must save what we can from the oncoming storm. It's *sauve qui peut* and salvage whatever can be rescued.

"I repeat: have not girls done as much for the doll?—the doll—yes, target of things past and to come? The love of the last doll was foreshadowed in the love of the first. Scratch a girl—even a very little girl—and you're sure to find a decorator! You can spot it from the first moment she wishes her room had yellow wallpaper instead of blue, a yellow carpet instead of beige or from the day she decides to move the chairs around to clear a space for her Ouija board experiments. It's a yearning that starts with doll houses and usually goes on for the rest of her life!

"I ought to know, for I started with a doll house myself and have grown-up to be one of the country's leading interior decorators and philosophers.

"When I was a doll in London, the only doll with a heart, a Jewish rag picker found me and sold me to a young Italian boy who worked the streets as an organ grinder. The boy's monkey had sickened and died not long before. Despite the boy's pleas, the rag picker had refused to stuff the dead monkey. But, as recompense, the rag picker gave me to the organ grinder so that I might play the monkey, play in the place of the dead monkey, as the boy worked the streets with his barrel organ. Oh, the times..." The speaker loses himself in recollection and falls silent.

He takes off and wipes his spectacles before going on.

"For wall-to-wall carpeting for your doll house: use toweling.

"One. Cut a brown paper pattern of the floor of the rooms to be carpeted.

"Two. Pin pattern to the toweling and cut toweling around the edges of the pattern.

"Three. Lay loose in the room or secure in place with 'dots' of glue under each corner of the carpet.

"For area rugs: use wash clothes cut to size.

"For the walls use any well-scaled (not too large-patterned) wallpaper, or use fabric or wallpaper to match the curtains, which is of course an excellent way to bring color and pattern into the room.

"A screen is a practical addition to any room and always adds an elegant touch.

"One. Take the cover of a gift box (or any part of the box)—cut out a flat piece of four inches by five inches.

"Two. Using a ruler, start from left and mark off three 1-inch spaces on the top (a) and bottom (b). Mark off four 1-inch panels by drawing straight lines from (a) to (b).

"Three. Using a metal-edge ruler as a guide carefully and lightly draw an X-Acto knife along the ruler's edge down each line you have drawn. Be sure you do not cut all the way through.

"Four. Fold the first panel forward (on the a-line). Fold the third panel back, in the opposite direction (on the b-line)—and fold the fourth panel forward (on the c-line).

"Five. When you have finished, press all the panels together firmly—and the screen will look like this." The philosopher-decorator holds up a miniature screen.

"Six. Cut a piece of floral or stripe contact paper 4 inches x 5 inches and paste it on one side of the screen. Then fold all the panels together again. Very tightly.

"Seven. Gently open the folded panels—and you have a screen that will stand by itself.

"For a doll house to use a real house as its model, use a 'scale model,' with a scale of three-quarters of an inch to one foot, which means that your doll's new home will be built by using measurements used in building a real house."

All these abrupt shifts between practical and speculative the audience attributes to the difficulties of conjoining philosophy with decoration and to the challenges, rigors, and unexpected defeats of the interdisciplinary endeavor which today's speaker has labored at since that long-ago moment when he first wished the wallpaper in his bedroom were yellow instead of blue.

"The story is told of an automaton constructed in such a way that it could play a winning game of chess, answering each move of its opponent with a countermove. A puppet in Turkish attire and with a hookah full of hashish in its mouth sat before a chessboard placed on a large table. A system of mirrors created the illusion that this table was transparent from all sides. Actually, a little girl who was an expert chess player, quite a *Wunderkind*, sat inside and guided the puppet's hand by means of strings. One can imagine a philosophical counterpart to this device. Inside the little girl, the *Wunderkind*, there was a doll, the true expert on chess. This puppet-girl-doll called 'historical materialism' must win all the time. It can easily be a match for anyone."

When the speaker pauses once more, a hand shoots up.

"Consequently," asks someone, indistinguishable in the back rows, "we would have to eat again from the tree of knowledge to fall back into a state of innocence?"

"Of course," replies the philosopher-decorator, "that is the last chapter in the history of the world."

Seemingly to underscore his point, although just how the audience does not altogether grasp, the philosopher-decorator takes a small wind-up toy out of the breast pocket of his suit. He sets it down on the podium. Its torso takes up the length of its body and it has wings that stick out clumsily on either side of its torso, like jug ears on a comic face. It could be an angel, an unexpectedly goofy one, or it could be a somewhat unattractively anthropomorphic insect. Whatever it represents, it's touchingly ugly. The philosopher-decorator winds up the small toy. Its wings flap—whir! whir!—as it begins to move backwards, almost as though it were attempting to levitate. Still earthbound, once it reaches the end of the podium, the toy falls onto the floor. It lies there like a beetle on its back, tin wings flapping—whir! whir!—while a grinding sound comes from its mechanism.

The philosopher-decorator shrugs. There's another whir! whir! before something gives and clockwork parts, like tiny cubist jacks-in-the-box, jump out of the toy.

The philosopher-decorator bends down to scoop up the broken angel-insect, giving it a look of astonishing tenderness before stuffing its dangling mechanisms back into the breast pocket of his suit.

The audience applauds, incomprehension masquerading as enthusiasm. They don't know that they're dolls, the speaker thinks, pityingly. They never do.

As he walks off stage, somewhat jerkily, one sees, for the first time, that he stands exactly twelve inches tall, that he has an old-fashioned wind-up key in his back, and that the string of a voice box is visible at the back of his neck.

Chapter Six: Little Lord Fauntleroy

Even though we meet through an online personal ad, it's not sordid at all, not squalid like anything those grown-ups do, not like what those real people get up to, because he's Little Lord Fauntleroy and I'm JonBenet. Since we're both dolls living in a work of fiction, I don't even know if I should say the usual things about persons living or dead, fictional or not, plastic or not. Anyway, consider the disclaimer made: all resemblances are purely artificial and wholly coincidental.

When, after a long email correspondence, we meet in person at last his manners are so good that it *is* delightful to make his acquaintance. I see a graceful childish figure in a black velvet suit with a lace collar brushed by love-locks of auburn waving about the handsome manly little face, whose eyes meet mine with a look of innocent good fellowship. If Boulder is a place in a fairy story, it must be owned that little Fauntleroy is himself rather like a small copy of the fairy prince, though he seems not at all aware of the fact, and perhaps is a rather sturdy young model of a fairy. His greatest charm is his cheerful, fearless, quaint little way of making friends with people. I think it arises from his having a very confiding nature and a kind little heart that sympathizes with everyone and wishes to make everyone as comfortable as he likes to be himself. Perhaps he has grown this way because he has lived so much with his father and mother, I find out, who have always been loving and considerate and tender and well-bred. He has never heard an unkind or uncourteous word spoken at home; he has always been loved and caressed and treated tenderly, and so his childish soul is full of kindness and innocent warm feeling. He is such a little man. He is one of the finest and handsomest little fellows I have ever seen. His beauty, indeed, is something quite unusual. He has a strong lithe, graceful little body and a manly little face; he holds his childish head up and carries himself with quite a brave little air. He seems to be a very mature little fellow. Such a beautiful, innocent little fellow, with his brave, trusting face!

I could go on forever, since this is love at first sight, but I'll just say that I'm charmed by his curls, his suit, his splendid manners. We have tea in miniature cups and he's impressed, he tells me that I'm so bold as to try Lapsang Souchong. When he invites me to his apartment, which is within walking distance, I hesitate winsomely, but soon I'm seated, feet dangling, on his couch of gold crushed velvet, listening to Japanese pop music. Screens add an elegant touch to his doll house and Japanese pop makes the perfect soundtrack for the perfect pair we make: two toys on a first date, JonBenet and Little Lord Fauntleroy.

He mixes up cocktails that are just the right size for us and taste like bitter candy, the bitterest candy you've ever tasted. Yummy. I talk about Des Esseintes from *À rebours* and how he played with music and liquor, trying to get the taste to match the sound. I don't want to seem overly bookish (please don't interfere now, Kathy Acker!), but I also mention the pianocktail in Boris Vian's *L'écume des jours*, which, when played, would conjure up a cocktail to match the music exactly, just as we are matched, exactly. We listen to Fantastic Plastic Machine in silence for a spell, taking child-sips of our cocktails, and imagining together that they taste like the sound of pop. I know he thinks that I'm well-read.

Later, I go to his balcony, which overlooks the Boulder Creek, to smoke one of my cute pastel-colored doll-sized cigarettes, and he follows me. He asks me if I'm nervous—such a well-bred little fellow! I look at him closely, blow a little O of smoke and say yes, I'm nervous and I'm only nervous when I have expectations. Inevitably, I've rehearsed this dialogue because there's nothing I hate more than spontaneity, for I am a doll, after all. When we go in, he gently and courteously caresses the green velvet that I'm wearing, velvet green against the gold couch, velvet green against his black Fauntleroy suit. It's not at all as though he were groping me, which makes me decide to break curfew and stay out. I tell him that the buses will soon stop running, and with the seamless transition of doll play or dreaming, he asks me to spend the night. I pause.

I waver just a bit, but long enough for him to repeat what he's asked. What's a doll to do? Soon we're snuggled up in his little boy bunk, and my face is up against his sturdy, handsome, manly little chest. Our hands explore the smoothness between our legs, and when he slips off the last of my underwear, I'm naked and blue and white just like the model of the dead little girl in that made-for-TV-movie autopsy scene. If you could only see us: we're bluer and prettier than Louis Quinze cherubs and a miracle match; we'd titillate your most rococo taste buds. Old Humbert Ho-hum may have had only words with which to play, but Little Lord Fauntleroy and I have one another for toys, nymphet and faunlet, supertoys to last at least all of a Boulder winter and spring long.

He declares that he wants to run away with me to Vegas and get married. It's tacky but funny and well-bred all at once, so I giggle an immaculate giggle. Silly boy doll. Of course we can't do that. They'd never let dolls marry, even Little Lord Fauntleroy and JonBenet dolls, even in Vegas.

As we fall asleep, my tiny hands touch his plastic body all over while I wish I had micro-miniature cameras in my hands like some really special Japanese camera doll, because then I'd photograph his artificial epidermis, so that the exquisite fake prints of his make-believe body could be stored forever in my little hand-cameras. That's the most a doll like me can hope for as memories, as souvenirs. I can hear the sound of the Boulder Creek outside his window and it's a night of a full moon. The rushing water is white noise, like a rain machine or one of those desk-top fountains that grown-ups use to make themselves feel calm. How stupid and silly they can be. I'm terribly nervous but utterly numb all the time. I take doll Valium.

I wake up in the middle of the night and slide my doll mouth onto his doll crotch, but he's not very comfortable, shocked a little, perhaps, so I stop. So what if Little Lord Fauntleroy is slightly sexually repressed? He is handsome and manly and well-bred.

The next morning we wake up to a postcard landscape of snow, even though it's early spring, and there's Boulder, always a snowglobe. He makes me black currant tea which I drink from a cup tinier than a fairy thimble. Then I have to take the bus home, my perfect body slightly sore from contact with a boy's, even though he is a doll like me. Can boy dolls give you razor burn? It's not unpleasant. He shaves his little boy doll chest, because otherwise his fencing outfits—yes, he fences! just like a real gentleman!—would chafe his naturally hairy little boy doll chest.

That evening I call him on my little princess phone. "*Tu me manques*," I mouth, knowing how sexy French is, even for dolls. "*Mais tu es charmante,*" he replies at once, and I am charmed, very charmed, altogether enchanted. What a fine fairy tale this is turning out to be! I forgot to tell you about his doll orgasm, because there's nothing to tell, really, except that it was perfect. He's so well-programmed. I'm a slightly different brand of doll, so I can't come on a first date. When I tell him this, he's delighted because he knows it makes me special. It's as though I were being removed from my box for the very first time.

After that, all our dates are velvet and cocktails and tinkling Japanese pop. I buy him gifts, like flowers (fake) and the smallest cufflinks in the world to go with his little boy suits. We always stay indoors. We never go outside. It snows almost every time we meet, big gustfuls of styrofoam snow. I spend the night in his bunk each time. We don't touch the smoothness between our doll legs anymore because he whispers to me, seductively, that it will be better if we wait.

I want it all now, but he's so persuasive, Little Lord Fauntleroy, and so charming, and so stubborn. His star sign is Capricorn and he speaks several languages fluently, such a clever toy: twenty-seven languages, to be exact, including languages ancient and modern, dead and alive, Eastern and Western, and even Esperanto. At least, that's what his instruction manual tells prospective buyers. It's not very long before I find myself murmuring in English, "I love you," into his handsome and manly little chest. "I know," is all he whispers back. I have to ask, "Do you?" and add, "I don't mean know, but do you, well, love me?" because I'm programmed to be insecure, perfectly insecure. "I don't tell anyone that I love him or her," he cautions, "I just act in love." It's bitter and romantic and like candy, and I could drink cocktails forever when I hear that.

If I'm created to love, I'm also capable of hate, but such details can't detain us, they can only foreshadow, like looming machinery, like plot mechanisms, like dark Satanic mills of narration. And who can tell perfection from its look-alikes, like death, or from its opposites?

In addition to my capacity for love, I'm very honest, honest at any rate for a doll. I have to confess to him that he's not the first, human or doll. Like the Little Lord Fauntleroy that he is, he simply declares that he doesn't care in the slightest about the dolls or humans, boys or girls who came before him. What a perfect little gentleman! Indeed, he reveals to me that he thinks of himself as a gentleman above all. He identifies, in particular, with Mr. Darcy in *Pride and Prejudice*. I would never have expected the intrusion of Jane Austen into our story, but fiction will be fiction. Still, I'm ever so slightly at a loss, especially since I can't quite recall what Mr. Darcy does in *Pride and Prejudice*, and naturally, I'm far too embarrassed to admit the shortcomings in my Jane Austen experience to Little Lord Fauntleroy. (Why doesn't Kathy Acker help me with this one?) Instead, I go to the public library the very next day and look up *Pride and Prejudice* in the Encyclopedia.

The Encyclopedia tells me the story—Mr. Darcy appears aloof and arrogant and standoffish, but he's the perfect gentleman. Hmm. "Captivated by Elizabeth Bennet in spite of himself, Darcy proposes to her in terms which do not conceal the violence the proposal does to his self-esteem..." Is he captivated by me? Has he proposed? Does this do violence to his self-esteem? I'm puzzled.

Boy dolls can be very hard to understand. I have to ask him what he means by being such a gentleman, by having such easily pained self-esteem, by turning into Mr. Darcy. "Always tell the truth," he admonishes, "and always put the other person before yourself." I have to tell him that I'm not a gentleman, only a girl doll, but he kisses me and reassures me that it's quite fine: he's more than gentleman enough for both of us. What a perfect little fellow! Handsome and manly! We should run away to Vegas. Imagine their faces.

He's Georgian, he asserts. Whatever can he mean now? Georgian, like a square brick building from the eighteenth century? This time, I know my definitions—"Georgian... when Palladian principles of classical proportions were adapted to an unpretentious, refined, and discreet style suited to the needs of the rising middle classes"? No, Little Lord means Regency. He worships Beau Brummell. But the Lord is no rake, I realize, when I ask what is the most sordid thing he's ever done (why do I ask such odd questions?) and he tells me that he's dated six other toys at the same time.

He tells me that he's often come home to find the doll with whom he's in love, right there, cheating on him with some other toy. Is it cheating that tells us love is a game? I want to giggle, but I don't. I should, though, because he's just given me the way out. JonBenet always needs a way out, a getaway, an escape route, an exit. That way I feel less trapped under the Colorado sky. That's why I keep the key to my diary around my neck: to pick the lock, to unlock whatever trap I might get myself into.

We never go out, Little Lord Fauntleroy and I. We spend all our time in his apartment, drinking cocktails with names like PixieStix and Tinkerbell as we listen to Pizzicato Five. It snows well into early summer and full moons come and go like clockwork, like clockfaces, and the Boulder Creek ripples past his apartment like shot silk on a puppet theater stage.

He loves *The Tale of Genji*—do I know that "Murasaki" means "purple," he wonders. Wasn't Lady Purple a bad puppet? I ask, for I recall reading *The Notorious Amours of Lady Purple, the Shameless Oriental Venus*. "See how the unappeasable appetites of Lady Purple turned her at last into the very puppet you see before you, pulled only by the strings of lust." "Silly, that's another story," he corrects me, and more than correcting my textual mixup, he is showing me that he does not approve of the strings of lust and he would he never obey their pull.

As we bow our little heads together over the large purple-bound copy of *The Tale of Genji*, he smiles. "What would we do if there were not these old romances to relieve boredom? But amidst all the fabrication, I must admit," he murmurs quite close to my ear, "that I do find real emotions and plausible chains of events." And he turns speculative: "We can be quite aware of the frivolity and the idleness and still be moved. We can be quite sorry for a charming princess in the depths of gloom. Sometimes a series of absurd and grotesque incidents which we know to be quite improbable holds our interest, and afterwards we must blush that it was so. Yet even then," he muses, sipping his cocktail, "we can see what it was that held us." And with a flourish, that is a small challenge to me, he adds, "I think that these yarns must come from people much practiced in lying. But perhaps that is not the whole of the story?"

"I can see that that would be the view of someone given to lying himself," I respond tartly, as tartly as lemon candy. "For my part, I am convinced of their truthfulness."

But Little Lord Fauntleroy has his own suggestion: "Suppose the two of us set down our story and give the world a really interesting one."

"I think it very unlikely that the world will take notice of our curious story even if we do go to the trouble of setting it down." I have to hide my face in my sleeve. Smiling and playful, he presses nearer yet. "Our curious story? Yes, incomparably curious, I should think." Yet, for all our allusive play, somewhere a narrator still worries, almost like a grown-up. What is to become of us? The cocktails are so sweet that only dolls like us can drink them, and so bitter that only toys like us can stomach them.

We watch the anime version of *The Tale of Genji*. "All art aspires to the condition of anime," I murmur, even though he doesn't appreciate the justness of my epigram. Our eyes are big as saucers, fearsomely cute, indisputably adorable, even if not Japanese-made.

He gives me a copy of *The Tale of Genji* bound in purple silk for my birthday, and he writes something in Japanese inside. "What does it say?" I ask. "It's the lovers' vow," he answers, "repeated throughout the tale: 'I shall love you in this life, and in the next, and in the one after that.'" We pause. "Even though I don't believe in reincarnation myself," he adds. No reincarnation—whatever does he mean? We're in fiction, which is the best kind of reincarnation there is. Sometimes we just don't seem to be in the same story; sometimes we just don't seem to be on the same page.

He doesn't like sex much. Perhaps he doesn't quite approve of it. He wants me to be monogamous to which I say yes only after another cocktail, while thinking about the next. I love to get tipsy, and since I don't ever eat, I'm often quite intoxicated. The times we have! Although we never go out, it's as if the whole world were inside his little apartment: all of Europe, all of Asia, inside a boy doll house in Boulder, Colorado. Why do we never have sex? Maybe he is like Mr. Whatshisname, Darcy. Never mind. We'll fall asleep in his tiny bunk, lovable as Babes in the Wood, pretty and almost dead beneath a leaf-drift of grungy blankets. Outside it snows in spring in Boulder, and sometimes it feels as cold as if it were snowing inside, too.

Our eyes are green: two pairs of green eyes, greener than the velvet I wore on our first date. His light up with brilliance. I think he must have a special battery. Mine go gray or blue sometimes. Mood ring eyes, he teases, and I giggle. "Another cocktail?" My eyes are mad mood rings. But when will he perceive only too clearly that my deathly pale wax face has no eyes, just black caverns where eyes should be; that I am a lifeless doll? If my eyes seem strangely fixed and dead, he simply needs to peer more intently to see moist moonbeams shining from them. When dolls desire the real, they see each other as dead and lacking; perhaps he loves me enough not to want me to be real.

We email each other, an entire miniature epistolary novel by email. I'm worried, because even though I haven't read enough Jane Austen, I have read enough to know that novels told in letters never have happy endings.

Would you like to see one of his letters? It's a letter about Japanese ideographs. I'll let you read it, if you like. "Maboroshi," says the header and the letter goes on:

as defined lexically: pre-modern
Japanese noun, first usage found late 8th c.

A. glossed by the sinograph *huan* (deceive, illusion) and the definition: "neither visible nor invisible, neither extant nor non-extant";

B. mid-Heian usages as "phantasm, illusion," almost exclusively found in prose;

C. by extension, late prose and poetic usages as "wizard, magician";

D. by further extension, late pre-modern usages as "ghost, spirit of the departed": said usages survive in modern literary prose and non-standard colloquial dialects (esp. Kansai/Shikoku subdialects, notably Awaji/Takamatsu and Hyôgo.

Like a maboroshi, you appear and disappear, my dear soul; our conversation as we lay beside each other in the dark, snow wavering outside.

The flowers sit on the counter in their glass, the whisky naps in the cupboard. Here and not here, present and absent.

Phantom.

Then he signs himself with an initial: F.

Silly Little Lord Fauntleroy, with all your talk of hauntings, get real! Don't you understand we're not real? How could we be? We're neither visible nor invisible, neither extant nor non-extant. We're phantoms of letters, to be sure, JonBenet and you, Fauntleroy (and yes, even you, dear reader, for having read that letter.) We're ghostly as the two white roses I gave you, insubstantial as spirits in the bottle. Has he guessed that I'm departed? Has perfection misled him into wanting what's real?

Everything, for the time being, still stays perfect in our snowy little world. No need for a narrator to worry over what's to become of us. Little Lord Fauntleroy goes away and comes back; I go away and come back, like clockwork, like full moons. While I'm away, I send him the smallest postcards I can find, covered with tiny writing. I tell him how Franz Kafka found a little girl crying her eyes out at a seaside spa. She'd lost her doll, that was why she was crying so bitterly. But Kafka told the little girl that her doll wasn't lost, just on holiday, like the little girl. For a long time afterwards Kafka sent the little girl postcards from her doll. Even Kafka could be a doll. Everything's perfect.

What draws me to him? We're each other's lodestars and lodestones, since he's perfect and I'm perfect. It's only logical for us to expect that, together, we must be even more perfect than perfection. We show up how incomplete ordinary perfection is in our joined incompletion. How very perfect! Perfection alone seems so lonely, so he and I, we square it, to make it much more than perfect, two lonelinesses together. We're programmed for perfection, which isn't all that different from being programmed for destruction. We depend on each other; we prop each other up; we are props for the other. Does fiction depend on a self or does a self depend on fiction? We gaze into the green saucers of each other's eyes and see ourselves like Hummel figurines. Our eyes are those in Keane paintings, in Tezuka cartoons, where deep, deep inside each other's doll eyes, we see each other doll-sized. He looks into my mad mood ring eyes, but only death, the union of the perfect and imperfect, gazes mildly out of them.

What makes me tick? Kathy Acker, dead woman writer, ticks deep inside me, tick tick, like clockwork, tick tick tock, like a time bomb. "A program for perfection can only be a program for self-destruction. Only what is dead is perfect, and you're only perfect because you're dead, JonBenet," mutters Kathy Acker, grimly, somewhere on the inside. Sullenly, she quotes, "'The woman is perfected./Her dead/Body wears the smile of accomplishment.'" She's always quoting, dumb Kathy Acker! How I wish she'd shut up, for once. But she quotes and ticks away. I must complete, I must perfect, our incomparably curious story.

By now I'm sad and bored constantly. Little Lord Fauntleroy remains always the same as his eyes flash green predictability. He mixes cocktails with names like Cowslip, Peaseblossom, Green Fairy (like his eyes, like our two sets of doll eyes) and Mustardseed. He never has a dollgasm anymore. He insists that I leave my own doll house and my other doll friends and live alone somewhere else. I do that, since I'll do anything for him. I must live out our incomparably curious story, even if somewhere a narrator is now wondering, worrying, what's to become of her? Why is she doing any of this? I carry on, even if Kathy Acker has predicted, like any Bad Fairy, that perfection will spell disaster. Little Lord Fauntleroy and me, we listen to Pizzicato Five and sip our drinks.

By now, too, I have to have cocktails just to face his handsomeness and his manliness, his perfection. When Little Lord Fauntleroy isn't around I just drink plain old doll fluid on my own. I become bad-tempered. I feel neglected and stifled. It's all just me, he admonishes me, because I haven't freed myself yet. From what, I want to ask. We are dolls, remember, so being free doesn't mean anything. He seems to have forgotten this. But I can't say anything because I'm too well-mannered in my own way, my own JonBenet way.

He has a party. All the toys of Boulder show up. Noddy, Sadako, Pokémon, the Sailor Moon collectible figurines, even some of the usual Cabbage Patch leftovers. Everyone. He looks so handsome and manly in a Jil Sander Little Lord Fauntleroy suit. It's cocktails for everyone, when he's mixing. The toys get tipsy but not rowdy, because everyone's perfectly well-mannered when Little Lord Fauntleroy's around. He expects nothing less.

But, at his party, he barely acknowledges me. He hardly freshens my drink. Why? Why? Am I not pretty enough? Haven't I won enough beauty pageants? I'm consumed by self-doubt as I stare into the mirror of my unfreshened cocktail. How will I ever deserve the love, or win the attention, even, of the Little Lord? He has a title! He's too good for me.

"Why haven't you told anyone about me, about us?" I demand. "Because I'm a fiercely private individual," he insinuates, with a gesture, without words. I'm about to scream. I'm on the borders of the Little Lord's life: he's so self-sufficient, so self-absorbed, so passive aggressive. Isn't perfection in the last analysis passive aggression? His particular passive aggression makes me just plain aggressive, but I hide it, because passive aggression is as contagious as mononucleosis in a Boulder school. I'm too well-mannered, I've told you, as I keep on telling you.

The party ends. My drink is stale. The cocktail cherry lies at the bottom of my glass like a fat tear of blood, a ruby blob. And I've missed curfew again.

I leave Boulder for a few weeks. At last, I go back to the toys who are like me. Immediately we play the most fun games ever, and suddenly I do feel free, free as a doll, free from Little Lord Fauntleroy and the tyranny of his freedom, his self-satisfied self-sameness, his tireless perfection. When I return this time, I have to confess that I've played with other toys behind his back. "You'd rather be with any doll than me; you'd rather drink cocktails anywhere but with me," I shout, all manners gone. He wins me back, winningly. "You think you're damaged goods, but you're not," he assures me. I'd like to believe him, but how can I? I'm damaged goods, that's for sure, but his battery-powered eyes can't even see that. I've been removed from my box. My value as a collectible has been severely diminished; my value has, in fact, shrunk to the size of his tiny Boulder doll apartment.

If we ever ran away, where would we go? I realize that even by toy standards, Little Lord Fauntleroy never has much to say. "All will be well." "Be true to yourself." As you would be to your school, your guy or your girl, I think, bitterly, but hold back from saying anything. Besides, what is my self, the self of the JonBenet doll? "You think too much." To me, he says this, to me, the JonBenet doll! "You mope." He intends this as a compliment, so there's nothing to do but mope winsomely to please him. I would do anything to please him. That's what dolls do, that's why we're here, silly reader.

After I've told him about my games with the other toys, the ones who don't live in the Boulder snow village (snow this late in summer!), he pays me a visit, which he tells me, before coming around, is only a social call. "As opposed to what?" I want to ask but don't. He never touches me anymore. We watch the moon float full over the trees of Boulder, a picture from a children's book. You could almost see a cow jump over it, as the little dog laughs to see such fun, only the dish will never run away with the spoon now, in this story. It's perfect. I hate it. I hate him. As he leaves, he says, superior as ever, "You know, I can't run away with you until you love yourself."

Well! If a doll could love herself, I wouldn't need him, now would I, stupid old Little Lord Fauntleroy! I'm very drunk. I'm very hurt. I call him on my princess phone to tell him he's a condescending, patronizing bastard. He says, very quietly, "I think you should get off the phone now." I hang up.

I call him the next morning to let him know that although he's programmed to speak twenty-seven languages (as his manual shows), what he's said would be stupid in any one and all of them. "I think you should get off the phone now," he says again, very quietly. I hang up, call back, get his answering machine—how many times these past months have I gotten his answering machine while the full moons roll by like clockwork and the Boulder Creek ripples like cheap fabric in a school play? "Coward," I spit into the machine and hang up.

Later that day, I call him again, this time on my special Hello Kitty cell phone. He loves me, he declares, and he wants all this to go on. All what, exactly? I feel the tug of love, irresistible as a puppet string. "Can we see each other tonight," I beg. "I'll have to call you in a week," he responds, and adds, with his usual whispery lisp, "I'll have to contemplate everything that's transpired." Why didn't I mention the lisp before? Why didn't I notice the lisp before? Because he's Little Lord Fauntleroy. Even I'm taken aback. Programmed to perfection, he needs a week to compute my responses and his reactions to my responses.

"WHAT ARE YOU?" I scream as loudly as a doll can. I hear him lispingly whisper, "I am what I am." This is too much! He lisps even when not articulating sibilants! Were I David, the endearing boy android in *Super-Toys Last All Summer Long* and *Super-Toys in Other Season*s, I would flail about now, malfunction heart-breakingly, and probably eat spinach till I had to go to the repair shop. But I'm not, I'm only a girl doll, only the JonBenet doll, although sometimes I dream I'm Kathy Acker, dead woman writer. And this is no Steven Spielberg film, not even a poor adaptation of Stanley Kubrick's posthumous genius, but instead *Real Doll Life, True Fictions of Toy Worlds*. So what can I do when Little Lord Fauntleroy whisperingly lisps, "I am what I am"?

I do the only thing that a doll like me could do under these circumstances. I break the fiction and name things for what they are: reader, wouldn't you? Isn't this why the narrator has been worried? I scream into my special Hello Kitty cell phone: "YOU'RE LITTLE LORD FAUNTLEROY! DON'T EVER CALL ME AGAIN!"

I never see him again, not once. I'll never love myself. I hate myself. Isn't that the point of existence? Because I'm not real. But I don't hate myself as much as I hate him. Without him, I'm much less real.

And that's not bad at all. You see, though I might not love myself, there's still always room for self-improvement, even for a perfect doll like me.

Chapter Seven: How I Made a Monster Out of Love

Once I loved you, but you gave me so little that I had to make you up. Once I'd made you up, you no longer existed as such. You'd become my fiction, my invention, my doll, and of course I had to break up with you.

In another Boulder apartment complex, this one a few doors down, poor foolish Victor Frankenstein says goodbye to his creature of graveyard scraps and shreds. "I loved you so much, I wanted you to exist," he whispers, "but you gave me so little that I had to make you up. You were alive! Alive! But once I'd made you up, you were only a doll, so now I have to let you go." The monster rises, roars, then, obligingly, becomes diaphanous, like film projected in an overlit room. A single leftover tear spangles his disappearance. Frankenstein shrugs and leaves.

On an island in unmarked, unmapped tropical seas in the room next door to my sublease in Boulder, Dr. Moreau rants at his creatures. They cower, fearing the lash of his technology, of his rage. "I love you!" he shrieks, voice almost incomprehensible with accent and anger. "You give me nothing! I had to make you up! Every one of you!" The last he screams while glaring at the panther woman in particular. "But now that I've made you up, you're only my puppets! I MUST LET YOU GO!" There's brief consternation before the beast-humans dwindle to taxidermied marmosets and hamsters, creepy stuffed toys, eerie Beanie Babies with unresponsive eyes.

On the wild heaths of Brontëland, a couple of blocks closer to the Pearl Street Mall, Heathcliff curses Cathy. They are both breathtaking and over-the-top, Laurence Olivier and Merle Oberon turned Technicolor from too much feeling, as they whirl through a kaleidoscope of desire. They are exactly what one might wish to see while on Ecstasy. The overripe texture of their emotions displays itself to the onlooker, as though inviting her or him to caress it. "Heathcliff," Cathy cries, "I never died. I loved you so much that once I realized you were never going to give me anything at all, I invented you, little knowing that my passion would suffer a fate even worse than just being unrequited. Once I'd invented you, you stopped existing. Heathcliff, you're the one who's dead, for you never lived outside my invention." In disbelief Heathcliff clutches his chest, but his hand passes through his already spectral body. Cathy, in her turn, sinks to the solidity of heathland dirt, the occasional scrub tearing at her dress, dusty heather pricking her with the persistence of her continued presence, alone as far as the eye can see. The horizons of Wuthering Heights ring Cathy like faggots, as Sylvia Plath wrote, as Kate Bush sang, interrupted only by the familiar craggy profile of the Flatirons.

In the Gilman Hotel, in Room 428, a dismal rear room with bare, cheap furnishings and a discouraging view of those Flatirons, near the seafront of shadowed Innsmouth, which is between Canyon Boulevard and Arapahoe Avenue in Boulder, a familiar stoop-shouldered, lantern-jawed figure, crew cut hair parted on the left side, sporting a worn nineteenth-century suit, cradles a plush toy in his cold arms. He strokes it lovingly with his corpse-cold hands. Of exquisite, if mass-produced, workmanship, the plush toy is of a vaguely anthropoid outline, but with an octopus-like head whose face is a mass of feelers rendered in shiny industrial silk, a scaly, rubbery-looking body, done in a clever illusion of gray felt, prodigious claws, about five inches long each, made out of real rubber, on hind and fore feet, and long narrow wings behind made from bright lamé with wiring. Of a somewhat bloated corpulence, thanks to its ample plushy stuffing, this thing is instinct with a fearsome and unnatural malignancy. It's also irresistibly cute, particularly with its big shiny embroidered eyes peeping out winsomely between the mass of feelers. It's not eldritch at all but as lovable as a teddy. Any serious collector of plush toys would fork over good money for it in an instant.

Still, that does not explain why the stoop-shouldered man with the old-fashioned suit is rocking it in his arms like a child, like a lover. He's whispering to it, and weeping, so that one can only grasp snatches of words and phrases—enough, at any rate, to hear that he's speaking in a high-pitched New England voice.

"Ph'nglui mglw'nafh Cthulhu R'lyeh wgah'nagl fhtagn," the man sobs. "Once I loved you... gave me so little... make you up... no longer existed as such... my fiction... my doll... I had to break up..." No matter how many times the man repeats "Cthulhu fhtagn," the toy stays a toy, gazing back brightly at him with its big unblinking embroidered eyes that peep with a mass-produced mischief through its mass of feelers. It lolls, like a Muppet in crochet, lifelessly. The plush toy and the stoop-shouldered figure stay in their embrace as the sun rises and sets, rises and sets, through the window with the discouraging view of the Flatirons in shadowed Innsmouth, which is between Canyon and Arapahoe in Boulder.

About suffering they're often wrong, the old writers. No tappings at the window, which I can smash to grasp your spectral hand, through which I can try to saw that ghostly hand on broken glass, to keep then as a paperweight. No colors out of space, no shadows out of time, no resurgence of the Old Ones rising from below the oceans where they have lain dreaming for aeons. No insurrection of my beasts, no smashed laboratory, no reversion into feral lusts. Not even a trail of corpses, to incriminate me, to remind me that we are bound forever, inventor and inventee. Not even a fucking phone call. "Hi, this is your monster, wondering how you're doing, sorry I've been so out of touch, let's get together sometime when my schedule's less hectic." Not one single goddamn postcard. "Sorry things didn't work out, but, you know what, if you go around inventing lovers, it's bound to backfire. But we can still be friends. Let's stay in touch. Best, your creature." Not an email. Still nothing.

You gave me so little. I loved you so much. Was it wrong to make you up? Why weren't you real when my considerable powers of invention, my scientific genius, my pent-up, womanly passions, homegrown on the blasted heath, my sexual ambiguity, my latent homosexuality, my undiagnosed transsexualism, all went into making you up? I'm not real, but I've invented you, which means that you're the toy of a toy, the fiction of a fiction.

I write to tell you goodbye, my doll, my beast, my monster. But you're words on paper, an overexposed image on a screen, something that becomes blanker by the second so that even "goodbye" cannot catch you in time. You've vanished before I could explain myself, explain you, explain us. And that's why making love is making a monster.

Once I loved you. When I loved you, I was trapped, for you knew that if I truly loved you, you could give me nothing at all. Fiction takes the place of nothing at all, so I made you up. Made up, all there was to do was break up. A voice in my head—whose? Kathy Acker's? JonBenet's? O's?—murmurs with authority: "Thus it will be forever with making love and making monsters: we invent."

Chapter Eight: The Synnot Children

These are my memoirs. Mine!

My memoirs are the memoirs of a doll ghost girl, ghostwritten by a dead woman writer, who may or may not be trapped inside of me, just as I may or may not be trapped inside of her, while the one clear thing is that we're trapped in Boulder, but where, I ask you, is Boulder, exactly?

Still, today has been a wonderful and strange day even for these memoirs, which may not be memoirs at all, but real hand-painted photographs of the dreams of the Boulder dead.

It's been weeks now that my pre-school for the ghost doll children of Boulder has been planning a field trip, under very strict supervision, to be sure.

This field trip would take us to the Denver Art Museum and the exhibition of European masterpieces brought in all the way from Australia. Ms. Realism, our art teacher, insisted that this is the best way to expose young minds to the magic of Art, High European Art, all the way from Australia.

I had a feeling that only Little Lord Fauntleroy would enjoy this, but he and I never speak. He is too handsome and well-mannered and manly, that little fellow, for a doll ghost like me. Still, he likes his art, although he never did get anime or even animation, so of course he never got me. I'm not alive but I am animated, by animatronics, if you must know, and not by nasty computer graphic imagery.

Off we go today to the big yellow bus, in a neat line of the ghost doll pre-schoolers of Boulder, all of us perfect dead doll children, ghost doll children. Some of us show a little blue or gray or dirty green in patches, corpse-cold, corpse-colored, with a little decay, wear and tear, plain old rot, you know, the usual ghost-doll-child problems, all of us in less than a savory state. Some of us have eyes lolling on chubby but mottled cheeks, some of us have wiring dragging from us, some of us stagger around a little, missing a limb here and there. We do the Zombie Walk, but we're quite disciplined, as Ms. Realism often remarks. We're like a puppet version of *Dawn of the Dead*, for young and impressionable audiences. You'd be astonished at how many of us there are for such a very small town, but then children die in Boulder all the time.

The bus creaks and rattles and jolts its way out of Boulder, past the rows and rows of cheaply-built tract houses that tie Boulder to Denver, past the shopping malls (I bought my goth outfit in one), fleeting as an investor's hopes, tawdry as the dreams of stark cold capitalism, and this is what grown-ups consider real and alive. They can keep it, as far as we're concerned.

We get to the Denver Art Museum, which looks like a fairytale castle where Rapunzel is kept or where Briar Rose sleeps. Okay, I'm lying a little. It looks like every other building in Colorado—like an asylum, a hospital, a hospice, a prison—but a tough one, certainly maximum-security. It's a fortress for Art, to keep Art in. Otherwise, Art would run screaming in panic through the streets, like Dreams, stopping traffic, and we can't have that!

I wander a distance away from the other doll ghost children, with whom I don't really have a great deal in common. That's why Little Lord Fauntleroy seemed so different. I hoped we would forever be dolls together, but we were Not Meant To Be. The entire question of Being is suspended when you're a dead doll, but you get the picture. Perhaps none of us is Meant To Be.

All the other dead dolls are nicely wearing their little ear sets so that some Grown-Up voice can tell them what to think of the paintings.

Screw that.

Oh, I mustn't swear, must I. Excuse me.

I'm JonBenet. I make up my own interpretations.

I'm spunky and self-willed; I toss my head, spiritedly, a little pony incarnate, a touch standoffish, entirely lovable; I stamp my little foot, a little princess, in the unlikely situation where I don't get my way.

I always get my way.

Almost always, and that's all that counts.

I'm thinking of Little Lord Fauntleroy again in front of a Baroque *Hero and Leander*; he's semi-naked and corpse-gray, she's sad, poor lady, wearing a big stiff tapestry dress, heavy as a carpet, so that she can hardly make the Gestures You Make When You Find Your Boyfriend's Drowned. Ms. Realism told us the story on the bus and I just had to look at this first. Yes, Leander does look like a grown-up Little Lord Fauntleroy. Leander's dead, of course, which may be why his skin is just as pale as the artificial epidermis of Little Lord Fauntleroy. I'm imagining a clever game of dress-up in which he and I play Hero and Leander, with Big Baroque Gestures. Even though he's so squeamish about sex, I could make him strip and wear a towel, while I get to wear a carpet for a tapestry dress.

We never speak now. I forgot.

Then I hear it: voices rasping likes cicadas but nearly not there, just, only barely, above the level of what your ear can catch, even if it's a mechanical ear, singing, shrill as steely wind-up mosquitoes, sharp-voiced as castrated choirboy automata, almost inaudible, insistent.

A music box melody of tortured insects, minute metal buzzing sings:

"Come away, oh doll ghost child,
Away from Boulder, its humdrum wild,

With a Synnot hand in hand,
From a world more dulled with deadness
Than you can ever understand."

I turn around. A single painting hangs behind me. It shows three children, life-size, from the eighteenth century: *The Synnot Children*, painted by Joseph Wright of Derby, dated 1781.

The Synnot children sang to me!

I run to get a catalogue, struggle back—the book is awfully big for me—and read, from time to time looking up at the painting.

The painting, I learn, has "great charm." It shows the three children, Maria, Marcus, and Walter, of Sir Walter Synnot (1742-1821) of County Armagh. Marcus and Walter sport Van Dyck fancy dress, while Maria is wearing a humbler neoclassical costume.

The painting is like a big birdcage made out of costume jewelry, to trap your eye, intricate and sickly as an over-decorated cake, rosettes and buds of icing, to deceive your tongue.

Stagily, the children pose in a grove, like a shadow box, a shadow play of leaves around them. The proscenium arch of the frame embraces them a little too tightly, as a worried adult might. Every gesture they make starts and echoes another pattern: patty cake, patty cake of shape and movement. There's a real rococo birdcage inside the birdcage picture. Maria, Marcus, and Walter have let a dove out of the birdcage. Walter holds the dove aloft. The bird looks stuffed, long dead, as do the children. They are flawless, enameled automata, paste jewels for features, each one, Maria, Marcus, and Walter, a birdcage deceit herself or himself. Is this Arcadia? Death lives here, anyway. Caught in the middle of a forbidden game, which may be their own lives, the Synnot children look shifty. They know how to hide things in plain view, how to trap the eye and twist the tongue. Little hypocrites, they pose as the Angel Gabriel (Marcus) performing the Annunciation to Mary (Maria), with Walter as God the Father and the dead dove as the Holy Ghost. They're clever because what adult would ever think something could be wrong beneath such a pious play, little blasphemers.

I'm impressed.

They are my brothers and sister.

Again, they sing to me:

"Come away, oh doll ghost child,
Away from Boulder, its humdrum wild,
With a Synnot hand in hand,
From a world more dulled with deadness
Than you can ever understand."

I drop the dull, heavy catalogue and walk towards the canvas, which is rippling now, like a television screen filled with static from outer space, like a doorway to the world of two dimensions.

Maria says,

"My brothers and I are made out of Jordan almonds, shards of Sèvres porcelain, and the hair of dead grown-ups. Our movements ape a Holy Trinity. Walter is God the Father, don't you see? Our nails are long, sharp almonds, or dangerous splinters of clear glass. Everything in our world is fronded, scalloped, or pleated. Trees fall like drapes, leaves froth like lace, drapery twists like boles. Our hair curls like foliage, like embroidery. If only you could enter our space."

Marcus says,

"We're a music box that conceals unsavory evidence. We're a wedding cake laced with strychnine at a doll's tea party. We live forever in our frame with the dove we've killed. The dove of innocence, the homing pigeon that will never leave us. In eight years' time, they'll storm the Bastille; in eleven years' time, France will swim in blood. None of this matters to us. If you could only enter our space."

Walter says,

"We play the Holy Trinity, the Annunciation, so slyly. Have you worked out our charade? Do you know what we do when your back is turned? Our eyes don't follow you around the room, as stupid grown-ups imagine. How vain of them! No, we play something much better. When their backs are turned, we kill the dove. Our magic is that we can kill the dove over and over again, the Holy Ghost, the dove of innocence, because like us, it's made of Jordan almonds, Sèvres scraps, and a few feathers to make it look like a bird. Transubstantiation! Our Host is made of almond paste.

"We perform a Black Mass in pastel colors and porcelain and icing; we're a Hellfire Club for toddlers, who look a little like Baby Jane, awkward and bewigged. But no matter. If you could only enter our space."

Maria, Marcus, and Walter say,

"We live forever in our frame; we're safe in our world of two dimensions. If only you could enter our space. But you can't; you're shut out in the adults' world of three dimensions. Come closer."

Gosh, they've just predicted the French Revolution! Field trips in the Boulder School District are learning experiences! So what if their references are a little dated—they're beautiful and fake like me. I want to live in two dimensions too! I want to shed this extra dimension!

"I'm a dead doll, just like you," I say, defiantly. Just because they're British doesn't mean they're better.

"Yes, JonBenet," answers Maria. "Step into our frame; come with us to the second dimension." I hesitate.

What will Ms. Realism say if I vanish on a field trip?

"Dear JonBenet, doll ghost child, we must hurry," says Marcus. "You must beware that goody-goody Little Lord Fauntleroy. He's a prig. His self-righteousness seems like principle. His integrity merely dresses up self-justification."

"We're not even sure of his title," adds Maria. I'm not going to stand here and share ex-boyfriend stories with these children—I want to enter the second dimension! They're beautiful, my sister and brothers, and I want to live in two dimensions with them, even if their predictions seem a touch out-of-date.

"Let's not talk about Little Lord Fauntleroy," I reply, with a cute shiver of distaste. "He and I never talk; we'll never see each other again. But how can I enter your world?"

They don't reply. The rippling seems about to be still.

"There's something else, JonBenet," say Maria, Marcus, and Walter, together. "You are a dead doll, as indeed we are, but because you live in three dimensions, you're in danger. Dear JonBenet, we don't know how to tell you this. There are two deaths. Everything's doubled, haven't you noticed? You must see. One death is fiction—that's the good death. The other is real death, dying to be real. You must never, ever, die to be real. It's disgusting."

Their faces show revulsion; the canvas quivers and ripples one last time, before it's still.

But still I hear their voices,

"There are stories of a Blue Woman, the Governess, the Delegate of the Fathers, who makes dolls and dead children everywhere turn real. In other words, her kind and her kindness kill. Beware of her."

And they sing, perfectly settled in two dimensions forever.

"Come away, oh doll ghost child,
Away from Boulder, its humdrum wild,
With a Synnot hand in hand,
From a world more dulled with deadness
Than you can ever understand."

Don't leave me here with the likes of Little Lord Fauntleroy and this scary Blue Woman. Take me with you!

"Are you dawdling again, JonBenet?" scolds the voice of Ms. Realism behind me. "Pick up that catalogue and turn it in at the front desk! The bus is leaving right now!"

I step back from the portal to the Second Dimension. It has closed on me, shut me out, Paradise Regained and Lost, in one afternoon.

Back to Boulder, the bus creaks and rattles and jolts its way, past the rows and rows of cheaply-built tract houses that tie Boulder to Denver, past the shopping malls, fleeting as an investor's hopes, tawdry as the dreams of stark cold capitalism, and this is what Ms. Realism considers real and alive, "realistic." Back to school, back to the Tudor.

Someday soon, I'll be two-dimensional, too!

I am JonBenet. These are my memoirs.

I don't ever want to be real, never ever.

Chapter Nine: Why Stephen King Writes Such Bad Novels

The lecture today at the university, the flagship, the spaceship of Flagstaff Mountain, will be free and open to the public. Kathy Acker will speak on the topic of "Why Stephen King Writes Such Bad Novels." Already, the topic alone has drawn a small, Boulder-sized amount of controversy, because Stephen King once lived in Boulder and the town feels fond, perhaps even defensive, of its former inhabitant.

As she moves into the auditorium, shouldering a hefty tote bag stuffed with the literary output of Stephen King, all extensively stick-noted, and which she intends to use as proof, Kathy Acker tries to conceal a slight stagger. She's still a touch hung over from last night's Ecstasy. Is there something wrong with the Ecstasy in this state?

She's nervous, but once she sees the rows on rows of bland expectant faces, deer not only caught but taxidermied in the trenchant headlights of her intellect and anger, all apprehension dissipates. Aggression takes its place, along with a dull headache somewhere unspecific in her cranium.

She strides to the podium, dumps the tote bag, rummages in it, then gets out some transparencies for the overhead projector and several dog-eared pages, covered with her angular script. Her single long earring quivers with eloquence.

"You're here today to find out why Stephen King writes such bad books," she begins. The benign audience, braced for controversy, moves around a little, adjusting buttocks to seats, trying to reach the most comfortable sitting position in which to be shocked. The town of Boulder so enjoys a challenge.

Faced with their unruffled, unflappable tolerance, Kathy Acker finds that the dull unspecific headache is winning over aggression. She's losing her train of thought. Fuck. She should have prepared better; she'll have to improvise. She can do it. Time for some theater. She reaches down, hoists up the tote bag, pours its contents over the podium, from which they spill, weighty paperback novels by the score. When the paperback avalanche stops—a last one slides off the stage and into the front row with a dull plop, like a stuffed toy—spines are broken and books lie open in attitudes of defeat.

Eyes closed, Kathy Acker declaims:

"CARRIE A GIRL WITH A FRIGHTENING POWER!

CHRISTINE!

THE GIRL WHO LOVED TOM GORDON!

TWO DEAD GIRLS!

MISERY!

IT!

MY PRETTY PONY!

PET SEMATARY!

MISERY IT MY PRETTY PONY MISERY IT MY PRETTY PONY MISERY IT MY PRETTY PONY!!

CARRIE CHRISTINE TWO DEAD GIRLS CARRIE CHRISTINE TWO DEAD GIRLS!!

DEAD ZONE INSOMNIA DEAD ZONE INSOMNIA DEAD ZONE INSOMNIA!!

SOMETIMES THEY COME BACK!

SOMETIMES THEY COME BACK!

SHINING STAND STAND SHINING SHINING SHINING STAND STAND SHINING STAND SHINING STAND SHINING STAND SHINING SHINING SHINING!!"

A few heads nod encouragingly. Some attendees are scribbling notes.

Kathy Acker opens her eyes to glare at the note-takers and nodders.

She grabs the nearest novel and reads a blurb from its back cover.

"DON'T TURN YOUR BACK ON THIS BOOK!" she shout-reads.

The audience becomes a little jumpy.

It's time for Kathy Acker to score her point, time for a thesis statement like a bomb threat.

"That's right! Stephen King isn't just a bad novelist, crappy, derivative, moralistic, unimaginative, limited. He's a bad writer, an evil one. DON'T TURN YOUR BACKS ON ANY OF HIS BOOKS!! They're much worse than any of his so-called monsters or villains.

"Stephen King is evil like Boulder and Boulder is evil like Stephen King! Don't think I haven't seen through the little understanding the two of you have going on." She eyes her audience. Kathy Acker is in full swing. The audience settles back, willing, eager even, to be insulted.

"Carrie was murdered by Stephen King in 1974, the year before the last American troops came back from Vietnam," Kathy Acker declares. "Stephen King stole the secret of Carrie's psychokinetic energies and used them to further his own career! He took the arcane mysteries of girly magick for male ends, for colonialist aims, FOR BOULDER PURPOSES!"

She's got them.

"After America's defeat in Vietnam, the time had come to redraw the lines of the American Empire. As John Dee stood to Elizabeth I and the creation of the Empire of England, so Stephen King stands to the New American Empire, a court magus for totalitarian democracy. Stephen King was there, armed with his psychokinetic powers stolen from the murdered Carrie, psychokinetic powers to move space psychogeographically through time.

"This is the Third American Empire.

"Its precise location is right here in Boulder!"

The audience looks around at one another. The note takers have stopped to gape.

"But where, I ask you, is Boulder? Let me remind you of what Marlowe's Mephistopheles replies when Faust asks him how he can be outside of Hell, 'Why, this is Hell, nor am I out of it.' Boulder is Hell, is the Third American Empire, nor are we ever out of it."

She will force them to face her truth today, even if she has to make it up. Damn them, the headache thuds. But to where? This is already Hell. And Marlowe was just another Magus of another Empire, no more, no less.

"The works of Stephen King have allowed Boulder to replicate itself along ley lines, lines of energy and force, infinitely. That is how Boulder has come to be everywhere. King's work inspires emulation, mimicry, replication. When *The Shining*—a key Colorado text—was remade as a made-for-TV movie, a viewer at the premiere held in the Overlook Hotel lost control during the croquet mallet scene and started smashing the banisters of the Overlook. For once, King's game transpired a little too baldly. This was imitation exposed. As indeed the presence of the model of the Overlook inside the Overlook itself may seem to be.

"Oh, I'm not talking about anything as mundane as copycat violence. I'm trying to warn you about the insidious powers hidden in each and every one of these books to duplicate Boulder *ad infinitum*."

For emphasis, Kathy Acker kicks one of the obese paperback bestsellers at her feet. It flaps, like a fat bat, into the auditorium. There are mutterings of "Call campus security."

Kathy Acker realizes she'll have to hurry. The rest of her speech she delivers in a burst of machine-gun eloquence.

"But Boulder features in only two of Stephen King's novels, *The Shining* and *The Stand*, you say.

"All of Stephen King's work makes up a secret psychogeography of Boulder that allows this town to travel in multiple guises through time and space, turning one place into all places. In the Empire of the Snowglobe, we are all trapped inside the Overlook doll house model that is itself confined inside the Overlook Hotel. Yet we believe we are free and that Boulder exists in a delimited geographically real area. Fools!

"Why is it that the National Institute of Standards and Technology is in Boulder? Why is the ominous Atomic Clock in Boulder? To homogenize space-time *as* Boulder! Why is the National Center for Atmospheric Research in Boulder, encased in its I.M. Pei structure of enigmatic yet sinister occult design? Why do all the domestic buildings face the winter sun in Boulder? Why is there that stupid star on Table Mesa above Boulder each year at Christmas time? That's the evil star that announces not the birthplace of the Messiah as Boulder, but of Boulder itself as Messiah!

"Because Boulder consists of nothing but a debased solar cult that uses Stephen King's works to transmute and transmit everything into Boulder. The National Institute of Standards and Technology you must understand as the Institute for Americanized Nationalized Standards, just as the National Center for Atmospheric Research nationalizes and Americanizes the very atmosphere!"

A choking fit cuts off Kathy Acker's speech, which has risen to a shout. She chokes, she splutters, she gulps back water. She starts again, more frenzied than ever. Why don't they see?

"At first I believed that ugly carpets, bad domestic space, and yards of gravel and bark could account for Boulder. How naïve I was! My task today must be to explain Boulder AWAY, once and for all!

"It is not that Boulder models a larger reality, oh no, the larger national and global realities have become the model of a model. More, the relationship among the models has become unstable—I ask, is Boulder America or vice versa? Is Boulder the world or vice versa? If only I could impress upon you the significance of the snowglobe—while it appears only to be an innocuous model, the snowglobe must instead be apprehended as a model of the model, hence the ultimate reference point.

"Along ley lines leading from Boulder, modeled by the lines of campus architecture, refracted by the glare on the winter-sun-facing houses, channeled by the star above Boulder, directed by the lines of I.M. Pei's eldritch architecture, manifold duplicates of Boulder pass themselves on in the form of Stephen King's books. Why do you imagine so many of those books have been made into films? Have you ever wondered why Stephen King has a cameo so often in these films? OCCULT ENERGY TRANSMISSION!! PSYCHOKINESIS!!!

"The books and films, the multiple images of Stephen King, all realize and re-realize themselves as Boulder, although I concede that Boulder is protean. *The Stand* would have us believe that Boulder could be a haven for the saved at the end of days. The apocalypse has already happened! Hellmouth has opened and its gaping maw can only be Boulder! Boulder, red in tooth, ready to swallow all!

"America has always been a conspiracy theory and a piss-poor one at that, from the thirteen stars of the original states to the Salem Witch Trials to Whitewater to the War of Tourism to the War on Terror to fill-in-the-blank. This country isn't a participatory democracy, it's a participatory conspiracy theory. This country is no more than a conspiracy theory—an inane work of fiction that demands that you check your disbelief as you enter its borders, as you show your papers. Not to believe that America has the right to credence, not to believe that America exists, is a step in the right direction. All novelists are Stephen King and he is all novelists, just as Boulder is all places and all places are Boulder.

"The Great American Novel is nothing other than a conspiracy that permits the conspiracy, the belief in the great American Empire, to persist. BAN HIS BOOKS! *DON'T TURN YOUR BACK ON THEM!!* Don DeLillo, Thomas Pynchon, John Jakes, James Michener, David Foster Wallace, Saul Bellow, William Vollmann, Ernest Hemingway, Tim LaHaye and Jerry Jenkins, John Steinbeck, John Dos Passos, Philip Roth, John Updike, these are all the transparent pseudonyms of Stephen King! Engorged with boredom, tumescent with tedium—books like dull dicks, like blunt instruments. *The Human Stain*, I ask you? The Great American Novel equals The Closing of the American Mind—another shabby little conspiracy notion."

Sidetracked by her rage at the thousand faces of Stephen King—masks of dullness, each and every one—Kathy Acker allows herself a side note: "How absurd the collective dreaming in *The Stand*! What kind of narrative premise is that? I want you off those narrative premises!" Her own dreams flash back to her. She regains her stride.

"High art or mass art, what's the difference? A misdirection, a stage magician's trick! It's all scripted by Stephen King who himself is nothing but a ventriloquist's dummy for the Snowglobal Empire of Boulder! Don't believe in the Great American Novel—it's a ruse to have you invest belief in America!

"And belief is more energy. Ah, but the worst is that such multiple weavings, such cat's cradlings, of ley lines require substantial energy all the time, more energy than a debased solar cult or simple credence can give. The ley lines must be fed for Boulder to perpetuate itself. Where does this energy come from?

"HUMAN SACRIFICE! *HUMAN SACRIFICE!!* That's why Boulder is a college town—young people die so easily, so beautifully. A car crash here, a frat brawl there, a mistake with Ecstasy, a fight over a beer keg, the occasional unsolved campus murder case, dead kids, throwaways. Or rather, recycled, as Boulder prides itself on doing with everything, to make Boulder omnipresent.

"But even more—I must warn you that JonBenet will be murdered again, sacrificed to the Reality Principle that is Boulder. Or rather murdered for the Boulder effect: the Unreal that maintains steadfastly, arrogantly, unstoppably, that it is Real. Dolls with All-American values do not realize that they are dead, plastic shells of selves living here, and since here is everywhere, these good doll citizens have overrun the world. You say JonBenet is already dead, but I say, JonBenet will be killed over and over again just so that Boulder can keep on happening over and over, a recurring dream, the shape of our collective nightmares!

"MAKE IT STOP! Let us put our energies into causing the National Institute of Standards to levitate!

"If in that evil novel *The Stand* Boulder declares itself to be the Boulder Free Zone, let us then instead declare everywhere a Zone that will be Boulder-Free!! Only in doing so can we save JonBenet! Only in doing so can we cease suspending our disbelief in America-Boulder!

"FIGHT THE LIE OF BOULDER WITH FALSEHOODS ON MULTIPLE FRONTS!!!" she shrieks, banshee, fist in the air.

The audience recoils. Some are making their way to the exits.

Kathy Acker launches into a chant.

"Boulder Alabama Boulder Alaska Boulder Arizona Boulder Arkansas Boulder California Boulder Connecticut Boulder Delaware Boulder District of Columbia Boulder Florida Boulder Georgia Boulder Hawaii Boulder Idaho Boulder Illinois Boulder Indiana Boulder Iowa Boulder Kansas Boulder Kentucky Boulder Louisiana Boulder Maine," she pauses for a half-second sneer, since this is ostensibly the "home" of Stephen King but Kathy Acker knows better, "Boulder Maryland Boulder

Massachusetts Boulder Michigan Boulder Minnesota Boulder Mississippi Boulder Missouri Boulder Montana Boulder Nebraska Boulder Nevada..."

But her chant trails off as uniformed campus security guards surround Kathy Acker.

"No, ma'am, can't do this in Boulder. We have a law against levitating buildings. Or even conspiracy to levitate buildings."

As the security guards lead Kathy Acker off stage, the audience sees for the first time that she is exactly twelve inches tall and that the string of a voice box hangs down the back of her neck.

Chapter Ten: Tiffany Drowns in Ecstasy

Whenever Kathy Acker falls asleep on the dirty beige wall-to-wall carpet of her Boulder sublease—which is often, because the lack of oxygen at this altitude and the demands of breathing when you're dead beneath the snowglobe dome sky wear her down—she has the same dream.

That's why today she's writing it down in her black vinyl notebook with the sharp metal clasps, a notebook as full of dark promise or threatening come-ons as the most constraining of metal-and-vinyl corsets.

In the dream, she's considerably younger, sixteen years old. Just sixteen. To be precise, it's the night of her sixteenth birthday. She's having a small party for her twelve best friends from a Boulder Valley high school. (The friends don't matter; they're anonymous and as generic as highschool yearbook pictures, or buddies and confidantes in a teen movie or witnesses interviewed by a TV news crew. Only Sweet Sixteen gets star billing in the dream.) She's as pretty as a doll, lovable as a picture. She's a perfect girl-woman-child, caught in a freeze frame, forever young, never ill. If Dorian Gray were a Boulder teen, he'd be she. But sixteen-year-olds don't read Oscar Wilde in Boulder, so that reference must be Kathy Acker's interference.

She looks into a plastic fuchsia compact, which is heart-shaped, like most of her accessories (earrings, rings, pendant, prints on notepaper, everything almost). The other teens call her the Heart Girl. She sees nothing in the mirror, but if she could, she'd see that she has a heart-shaped face, winsome, the skin of a Barbie, strawberry blonde hair, wispily cut, waifishly windswept, held back from her face by tiny barrettes decorated with little bugs in multicolored glass beads and little hearts in pink and red rhinestones. Okay, it's a dated look, but what does she care? She's wearing a hot-pink tank top with the word PRINCESS in teeny rhinestones and the outline of a crown. She's wearing capri pants in pale pink with white polka dots. Her flip-flops are pink platforms with a poly-petaled daisy (retro-crazy) on the toe. Her fingernails and toenails are small rose quartz jewels shiny with special varnish. Her lips are moist with strawberry lip gloss, and a rosebud aftershower spray makes her pink all over. She's pink as a jewel, petals carved from pink jade, the inside of a kitten's mouth. Sixteen freeze-frame. That's what the face in the mirror would be; that's the girl who would live in the mirror, sixteen freeze-frame.

In her dream, Kathy Acker has to register that she, dead woman writer, Kathy Acker, would not be caught dead in this outfit, even if she were doing a Cindy Sherman send-up.

But the dream takes over, as it always does, and she forgets about Oscar Wilde and Cindy Sherman, and she's sixteen, a PRINCESS, the Pinkest PRINCESS in all the world of Boulder. She has strawberry blonde hair, and her name isn't Kathy Acker at all. It's Tiffany.

Tonight her sixteenth birthday is going to be very special, not just because she's sixteen and a PRINCESS, but because tonight she's going to take Ecstasy.

For the first time.

She's never taken drugs before, because she signed some DARE thing in high school that commits her to abstinence. Does that mean abstinence from drugs or sex? Probably both, because the DARE stuff always wants you not to try anything. Cigarettes will lead to marijuana will lead to acid will lead to teen pregnancy will lead to AIDS and then you're kicked out of the Promised Land of a Boulder high school and your Pink Paradise, because you sampled the Forbidden Fruit. Why is the Forbidden Fruit an apple, like something for the teacher? Why doesn't anyone ever think the Forbidden Fruit could have been strawberry or raspberry or some other rose pink berry? muses Tiffany, something wet and juicy like edible lipstick? But Tiffany's a good kid, jewel-pink, who'll do whatever's expected of her. Every time her parents ask her if she's taking drugs, she mumbles, "Yeah, right." But right away she feels sorry for being such a smart-ass and turns into Mommy and Daddy's little girl again, so she adds, before harm's done or feelings are hurt, "Oh no, I would never touch that stuff, how could you ever think that?" To herself she thinks, I'm Tiffany, strawberry blonde, and a PRINCESS in Boulder.

She got the Ecstasy from a friend of a friend, and just to show that she wasn't as unhip as she might look—but she's adorable! and only sixteen!—as she paid for it (with her very own money), she said, "I know I have to take lots of water with this, right," like she does this all the time and is just checking something she already knows by heart. And the friend of the friend, a scuzzy-looking guy in a T-Shirt that reads Raves-R-Us muttered, "Yeah, right, if you're like dancing all night at a rave," as he squinted up at her over the little stash of packages between his feet, where he'd put them once he'd got out of his van, with its "Rave-R-Us" and "NASA" stickers. It felt just like a drug deal in a made-for-TV movie, scary and exciting. Tiffany—excited, scared—glanced nervously over her shoulder back at the schoolyard—this was just about an hour after school let out—and replied, "Yeah, right, I know."

Then the Ecstasy, six pills wrapped as tight as a secret in tinfoil, like a shiny silver magic present gift-wrapped by fairies, was hers, like the gift a PRINCESS in a fairy tale would get on her sixteenth birthday. The Ecstasy is hers.

Wait. Kathy Acker wants to scream, don't you know what princesses usually get for their sixteenth birthdays? Haven't you read *Sleeping Beauty* or *Briar Rose*? How stupid, how badly read, are these kids in Boulder high schools and why is she one of them in her dream? Doesn't anyone understand foreshadowing any more? Wait. Kathy Acker, dead woman writer, lapses back into the comfortable dumbness of the dream. She's a she again. Tiffany, to be exact.

Her parents are out for the night. They know that Tiffany is a good kid who's signed a DARE pledge and would never touch drugs. Sex is out of the question, unthinkable. So they've gone off with a gruff "Don't do anything funny!" from Daddy and a worried "Be careful, dear, won't you?" from Mommy. Because she's sixteen—how quickly time flies—it must be okay to leave Tiffany alone tonight with her twelve best friends. And her parents write the number of the neo-nouvelle, post-fusion, molecular-foam all-you-can-eat restaurant they're going to, on the pad next to the phone in the hall.

The Ecstasy is hers, a fairy gift for a sixteen-year-old PRINCESS. As a joke, she puts on a little tiara of pink plastic rhinestones when her brother dims the lights in the living room. Someone turns up the music, and someone else brings in the birthday cake from the kitchen. It's an ice-cream cake, a lopsided business of bright pink frosting, and she just knows everyone's going to gorge.

She blows out the sixteen pink candles—rosy glow from candle-light on her sixteen-year-old face, cheeks puffed like a cherub—and wishes, like Dorian Gray, but without knowing it, that she could stay young and beautiful forever, just as she is right now.

And now it's time for Ecstasy. There's more of a hush now than when she blew the candles out. Her twelve friends crowd round her, ooohs and aaahs, nudgings and giggles, scrunched-up sixteen- and fifteen-year-old faces signaling, "Drugs are gross!" and how daring Tiffany is for trying anything like this. And they collapse helplessly into giggly sixteen- and fifteen-year-old heaps. Tiffany unwraps the six pills and puts them out on the sturdy southwestern-style oak of the dining-room table, in her parents' house in Boulder, Colorado. She arranges them into a small heart shape. Suddenly impatient, she pops one in her mouth. She's just sorry the tablet isn't pink, like cinnamon candy. Ooohs and aahs. "What's it like? Are you feeling anything? Hurry up and tell us!" Yet more giggles.

Nothing happens.

Ten minutes go by.

She takes another.

Nothing happens. She waits twenty more minutes for nothing to happen.

She's not going to let a jerk like that guy in the Raves-R-Us T-shirt ruin her sixteenth birthday. She gobbles up the last four.

With lots of water, every time, with all six, because she knows that she has to take lots of water. She has to avoid dehydration, like a Bad Fairy who might come to a sixteenth birthday party, uninvited, unannounced.

Nothing happens. Tiffany drinks more and more water.

Lots of water as nothing keeps happening.

And, eventually, nothing really happens. Nothing *does* happen.

That's the only way to describe it, it's so weird. Nothing is actually taking place, right there, in her parents' living room, on her sixteenth birthday, with her twelve friends crowding round her, now panicky, tearful nearly, some already red-faced, wet-faced with tears, pleading, "Tiffany, Tiffany, get up!" "Tiffany, Tiffany, can you hear us? GET UP!"

Nothing happens. It's ecstatic. Tiffany would like to giggle but she can't, she can't do anything except lie on the carpet of her parents' living room in Boulder, Colorado.

Slowly, very slowly, Something Happens in the middle of Nothing Happening.

Tiffany realizes that she's drowning in Ecstasy.

She's had too much water.

She's drowning, right here, on the carpet of her parents' living room, in Boulder Colorado, while the Boulder Creek rushes past outside.

The Creek rushes past like nothing happening.

Tiffany realizes that if she's drowning, she will die, that she is dying.

The Something Happening in the middle of Nothing Happening is that she is dying.

Her twelve friends are very far away. She sees their fifteen-and sixteen-year-old faces like high school yearbook photographs disintegrating in water.

She's a perfect girl, caught in a freeze frame, forever young, never ill.

The Bad Fairy has arrived. She has given the spindle-prick of Ecstasy as she does to all perfect girls. The Fairy has come to your birthday party, Sleeping Beauty, lost underneath wreaths and wreaths of pink roses, wave on rosy wave of flowers.

She can see the headline in tomorrow's *Daily Camera*: SIXTEEN CANDLES SNUFFED OUT BY ECSTASY!

Somewhere else, Kathy Acker stirs in her sleep.

When you drown in Ecstasy, the last thought you have is, this is not so bad. Or rather, when you drown in a suburban living room in Boulder, Colorado, from the water you drank, because you thought you should drink lots of water with Ecstasy, even though that's a scrap of drug wisdom, of urban lore that's usable only when dancing at raves or in clubs, and your parents' living room on your sixteenth birthday is no dance club, no clandestine or mundane rave, no strobed warehouse of X'd out partygoers, no place in which you can get dehydrated, so drinking lots of water makes you drown on dry land because the Ecstasy kicks out your natural physiological responses to drinking too much water, so you're not really drowning in Ecstasy, you're drowning in lots of bottled water you'd drunk because you took Ecstasy and the Ecstasy has stopped your body from registering that you've had too much water, so that you are presently drowning in your parents' living room, next to the sturdy southwestern-style oak dinner table, glimpsing your reflection in the TV screen, black as a witch's mirror, and on the beige wall-to-wall carpet, on your sixteenth birthday with your friends going, "GET UP, TIFFANY! YOU'RE SCARING US! WHAT'S WRONG? GET UP!" In a dim background you hear your brother saying, "I'm calling 911, man, this is bad."

Whatever.

It's not so bad.

Not *Sleeping Beauty* or *Briar Rose* anymore, the fairytale runs backward. You never wanted the Prince, so you go from human to mermaid, from real to make-believe, as you drown.

You become the siren and the sea.

You sink fifty thousand leagues or full fathom five to the bottom of the Boulder Creek on the carpet of your parents' living room.

You sink through water slick and iridescent, the peacock's fan of a petrochemical spill. In this poisonous rainbow, you even glimpse pink, your color, and you want to grab on to it, a twist of pink, but it's gone as you float ever downwards. You're in the Boulder Creek, which has opened into all the seas, all the oceans, all the bodies of water in the world. The tides whirl you around, drag you under, wash you up, pull you in, drop you down to bottomless depths. The waters shine with rich opaline toxins, heavy metals like moiré, a globally contaminated water supply blinding you with noxious moonstones and amethysts, poisoned hyacinths and delphiniums.

You're in the Boulder Creek, which has turned into a giant snowglobe held within the snowglobe of Boulder, a snowglobe that's a gigantic fish tank filled with thousands of tons of toxic glitter and spangles, shifting leisurely, dazzlingly, in every inconceivable color, like the mercury scales of a myriad fairytale fish, enchanted motes dancing in venomous otherworldly light, the radioactive tails of a million mermaids shimmering, flashing before vanishing, an avalanche of nuclear pixie dust borne aloft by dancing currents, in a tank stirred by giant mechanical devices moved by the slow motion of delirium.

What waste must have seeped into the groundwater to produce this unspeakable aquatic sunset under the seas, at the end of the world?

Strawberry blonde hair spread wide, Tiffany spirals down, post-nuclear Ophelia of the Boulder Creek, with its deceptive deeps. All the cinnamon and tourmaline pinks of coral reefs, all the rosy nacreous shades of the underwater, all the palest pink pearls of pirates' hordes go with her, as she dances to the bottom.

Only sixteen, Tiffany-Ophelia has no life to flash past, so flashes of others' drowned lives seep into her eyes, like a nuclear spill.

Skeletons with lilac and mauve sea anemones for eyes sing to her the wisdom of drowned women.

Skeletons with jellyfishes for breasts sing to her the vengeance of drowned women.

Kathy Acker moans in her sleep.

"Goodnight ladies, goodnight ladies.

"You are the siren and you are the sea.

"Take him down with you; make him drown in you.

"For you are the siren and you are the sea.

"Little Blue Sailor, Little Boy Blue, Little Lord Fauntleroy, his ship was just the Titanic in a bottle.

"Once he said, when you're drowning, you'll kick out at anything.

"Once he said, it just feels like drowning if you think you're the only swimmer in the ocean.

"Once he said, swimming against the current makes it seem like you're drowning.

"He was wrong.

"Take him down with you; make him drown in you.

"Take him down with you now, like a four-hundred pound manatee would a ninety-pound sailor, like a leaden submarine, like a diving bell to the depths of the ocean, never to rise again.

"He was wrong; he's lost.

"Take him down with you; make him drown in you.

"You are the chambered nautilus, the sigil of toxic waste.

"You are Moby Dick in the shape of a girl, you are Cthulhu, dreaming in his house at R'lyeh, you are the Kraken and Leviathan, too.

"Those are pink pearls that were his eyes. Look!

"He called you the Hyacinth Girl, but he was never Phlebas the Phoenician, nor was he meant to be.

"Take him down with you; make him drown in you.

"Little Blue Sailor, Little Boy Blue, Little Lord Fauntleroy, his only ship was a dead message in a bottle, and that bottle cracked.

"He was wrong about drowning. He was wrong about it all.

"That's why you must make him drown.

"He's drowning in used condoms, in bent and rusty needles, in E. coli which thrives like plankton, in crude oil, among penguins and seagulls, professional mourners already coated in funereal black.

"He's gone under for the third time in your Sargasso of Half Life, your Malignant Gigantic Fish Tank, your Seven Seas, poisoned each and every one, your Primal Nuclear Ocean. You!

"You are the siren and you are the sea.

"You are the mermaid with the mood ring eyes, fickle as tides, treacherous as undertows.

"Goodnight ladies, goodnight ladies.

"He was wrong.

"He is lost."

How does Tiffany see and hear any of this?

Because she's sixteen and perfect and dying on the gray-beige carpet.

She knows because her life—all sixteen years of it—does not flash before her; instead, Kathy Acker, dead woman, skeleton with jellyfish breasts and anemone eyes, siren, breathes all this to her underwater, the wisdom and vengeance of drowned women, in long garlands of quicksilver bubbles.

Tiffany's sixteen and drowning on dry land in her parents' living room.

This is stupid, is her last thought.

But it's not so bad.

And this is the dream that Kathy Acker has every time she sleeps on the carpet in her Boulder sublease, which is fairly often. She finishes writing down her dream in an angular handwriting, with urgent upstrokes, with semi-colons, periods, and colons that almost pierce the page. She locks the diary carefully, sighs, and leaves it close at hand. Dreams strike any time now: dreams of insufferable sadness. What can it all mean?

Whatever happened to the teenage dream, sniffs Kathy Acker.

She tries to shake the dead teen dream.

Time to score some X, she figures, to clear her head.

But all the Ecstasy in Colorado is probably poisoned, cut with petrochemicals, strychnine, nuclear dust.

She settles back on the carpet and goes to sleep. Soon she's dreaming again.

Chapter Eleven: The Doll Who Said, Yeah, Right

Spice Girl, space girl, showgirl, cowgirl, fin-de-siècle Parisian tart, modernist robot from *Metropolis*, Lady Purple with kimono on kimono, be-sashed, towering chignon full of bristly stickpins—in all JonBenet's extensive wardrobe of pageant costumes, there is one she loves more than any other. No, it's not some Kathy Acker outfit. The Kathy Acker™ doll she owns in secret is enough, and besides, everyone would just think it's a punk get-up. People can be so stupid in Boulder, thinks JonBenet. She's writing with a bright pink pen in her tiny pink diary, the one with plushy vinyl covers, like pink lips parted to whisper a bubblegum secret, the one that secures those secrets with its special heart-shaped lock. Its very own small heart-shaped key fits the lock, a key that JonBenet wears around her neck on a chain as wispy as gossamer, and as nearly invisible, which suits her fine. Today she's writing down the dream she has every time she wears her favorite costume.

What is her favorite pageant outfit?

It's all black.

She appears onstage while "Kiss Them for Me" by Siouxsie and the Banshees, with a melody as undulating, shimmering, and sinuous as a serpent under the spell of a charmer, snakes its way out of the church hall loudspeakers. No one really understands it on the pageant circuit, and the routine sometimes loses her points, but JonBenet doesn't care. She loves the outfit and she worships Siouxsie.

It's all black with a cape, or what might look like a black trench coat, long enough to sweep the floor. She wears a very big crucifix—she used to say cross, but they taught her to say "crucifix" instead—around her neck. On the crucifix is an especially gory Jesus, writhing and twisting, like a big angry insect caught on a pin. Terms such as "long" and "big" are, naturally, relative to JonBenet's adorably doll-sized frame. She bought the crucifix and the all-black outfit at her favorite goth store in the mall with her very own money.

Her eyes are big with Egyptian-style kohl. She covers her moppet hair with a black wig, straight, with bangs. The dress beneath the trench coat cape looks like a spider web of black lace, and JonBenet becomes the Littlest Bad Fairy, Cobweb, the Subverter of Queen Titania. Or the Blue Fairy, whose name is only whispered to scare doll children. JonBenet dances like a delirious drag queen in the syrupy slow motion of ecstasy. There are tiny black plastic spiders glued to the corners of her eyes. The judges and mothers are usually more than a little taken aback.

And every time she wears the outfit, she has the same dream that night. That's why she's writing it down today in her diary.

In the dream, she's a little older. She's grown-up, almost, to be the cutest goth doll in all of Boulder. Her perfect pout is outlined in black; below her black bangs arch her plucked black brows; her nails click like small black scarabs. Her entire wardrobe is black, with teeny teeny silver skulls and rhinestone spiders on everything. She goes to Boulder Valley Doll Junior High, with all the other toys and dolls who are battling puberty and the ennui of middle-class adolescence in the snowglobe of Boulder—it's dull, even for dolls used to repetition and routine.

Today's a school day, in her dream, like any other. The older JonBenet hums "*Kiss them for me, I may be delayed*," under her breath as she takes a last drag on her doll-sized black clove cigarette. The paint on her nails is chipping, she notices. Like anyone in this school even cares about fashion, she thinks. How can dolls be such jerks, such jocks? She might as well have gone to a Real School. She shudders. All the Cabbage Patch Kids are maturing into hippies, with overalls, bib dresses, Phish T-shirts, and the omnipresent Tevas and Birkenstocks. Or the occasional rebellious Insane Clown Posse dolls. The American Girl dolls and the Bratz are downright unmentionable, locked up in their own maximum security cliques. JonBenet feels another shudder coming on and looks down quickly at her own overly pointy black patent leather boot, toe as sharp as a switchblade.

The school is an architectural model. No, it's not a model example of school architecture, it's an architect's model, from the Matchstick School of Construction. With fake shrubbery and busily dotted clusters of plastic figures (for "Human Interest"), it's an entirely unconvincing version of American School Life in the New Millennium. It's also one of the best regarded schools in Boulder County, as JonBenet's grown-ups always point out, whenever she begs to transfer to art school. It's the victorious coupling of Planning with Pleasantness. No smoking on school property.

As she rounds the corner to her first class, she notices a teddy bear loping towards her—odd, the bear is losing stuffing.

"Run away, JonBenet," pants the bear.

"Why? It's a school day and I don't want any more trouble," the older JonBenet shoots back defiantly, with all the toughness she's picked up from growing up different in Boulder.

"Oh, it's awful," sobs the bear, one paw inspecting damage to his chubbily stuffed body. Yes, he's definitely losing stuffing.

"Those two, you know, the..."

JonBenet doesn't. Boulder Valley Doll Junior High boasts a diverse population of not only dolls, but soft toys—like Teddy—action figures, collectibles, and all manner of new toys that show up on the global market. It's an adventure in doll demographics. But it's deadly dull. May as well be the snowglobal market, thinks the older JonBenet. They're all the same, but I'm the only goth doll in Boulder Valley Doll Junior High.

"They're-going-around-shooting-the-Christian-dolls-and-the-Kens-and-Barbies," Teddy blurts. Then she sees Teddy's beady eyes get black with fear as he starts running again, away from her. She turns around to see what he saw, behind her, and there they are, two Alienated Jock dolls.

Alienated Jock dolls, JonBenet sneers inwardly. Why bother? It's as bad as that movie, what was it called? Oh yes, *American Beauty* with Alienated Cheerleaders. Even though JonBenet is pretty enough and angry enough to be an Alienated Cheerleader herself, she'd never give in. She's truly gothic, so she sticks it out. She rummages in her black vinyl coffin-shaped bag for her doll iPod crammed with dark soundtracks. Anything to pretend she's not here, anywhere except here.

"Here we go again," sighs JonBenet in her head. Another round of "Hey, little goth doll, what's the matter? Dipped in ink?" Or "Black cat got your tongue?" Or "Smile!" Or "Cheer up, goth doll!" (She really hates the last one.) They are such Wrestling Figurine wannabes, she sniffs.

Look, they even have guns today. Probably some NRA rally, although how dolls can go along with that kind of thing is past her comprehension. ADFG, American Dolls For Guns. All those silly action figures, and, once you think about it, GI Joe really still has a lot to answer for.

Wait—that's why Teddy was running! JonBenet realizes all at once that the school is entirely silent under the sunny Colorado sky. Oh no! Toy guns! The Alienated Jock dolls are armed. What's going on? That's why Teddy was wounded. Teddy was right: they are shooting dolls.

JonBenet turns on one short spiky heel and runs, gathering up her long black velvet skirt.

The school is built in toy size out of asylum-brown brick. In its restrained neo-classical Lego, it could double as the model for a non-denominational place of worship, an airy shopping mall, a comfortable minimum-security prison, a hospice, even, for dolls who are terminally sick with Reality.

Past two cautioning abstract caryatids of distressed chrome, through a glade of miniature plastic ficus trees, JonBenet runs. She's running surprisingly fast for someone in a dream, she realizes. Faded candy colors, beige carpets, the warmth of a motel lobby, the charm of a cautious mental hospital, all of this speeds past her. She runs out of the building and onto the main quadrangle.

Doll carnage. Piles on piles of broken toys. Several teddies. Lots of Cabbage Patch Kids. Weebles who wobble but who don't fall down are nonetheless noticeably worse for wear. All the Kens and the Barbies and the Skippers in school. Like a landfill of dolls. Doll parts everywhere. Stuffing everywhere. When you shoot a doll, does it die?

This is not death rock, JonBenet wants to scream, because she senses she'll somehow be blamed. All that black, they'll say, every day, and in such a lovely sunny climate too.

And she loves Marilyn Manson. What a doll. He has boy doll parts and girl doll parts. She falls into a fantasy about Mechanical Animals, odd-eyed creatures whose irises whirl like carrousels, into whose carrousel-eyes she could fall, to be whirled away, worlds away, from here.

These jock nerds have no taste in music and no style. They could have put drugs in the cafeteria food, anything but this.

She swings around. She doesn't want to see the wreckage. It's time to run home.

But they're there.

"Are you a Christian doll?" they ask.

This is too much.

Fundie dolls are the worst, another bunch of adolescent Cabbage Patch Kids. Hippies or Jesus freaks, like there's some difference.

"Are you a Christian doll?" the Alienated Jock Nerds with toy guns ask again.

Doll lips curling with contempt, JonBenet manages to sneer, "Yeah, right."

They are really far too literal. It's just because she's wearing her crucifix. Maybe she should have worn an ankh. Or that pentagram, but then the fundie dolls go on and on about "Witchy, witchy," and everyone's always asking her if she thinks she's Wednesday Adams or in the Church of Harry Satan Potter or something. JonBenet decides to stop paying attention to the two dolls who confront her.

But then the two Alienated Jock dolls shoot her. Her. Right there.

JonBenet crumples to the ground, her security blanket of disbelief at once suspended. Like suspension in school, as a punishment.

It doesn't hurt if you're shot when you're a doll inside a doll dream, just like it doesn't hurt to think that you're going to die in a dream. It's a false ending in a fiction.

"Am I dying," wonders JonBenet.

She looks down. Her chest has been damaged beyond repair. "I am dying," she whispers. "*Kiss them for me, I may be delayed.*"

Dying in a dream feels like finding out you're a character in a story made up by someone else.

But before she can die, she wakes up. Always.

"Kiss them for me, I may be delayed."

That's why she's writing it down today, this dream in which she's the only doll with the courage to say, "Yeah, right." What can it all mean?

JonBenet finishes writing down her dream in her round slanting childish handwriting, carefully dotting i's with circles, stars and hearts. She locks the diary, carefully, hides it in the tiny toy chest, and goes to sleep.

Soon she's dreaming again.

Chapter Twelve: I Solve the Mystery of My Death

What's going on here? I'm JonBenet, the doll. Why am I dead? Who killed me? How can I make them pay, bring them to doll justice?

The sad truth is although the market in detective novels is entirely saturated with generic instances, I can't rely on nice Miss Marple, foreign and fascinating Hercule Poirot, spunky Nancy Drew, or one of those popular, pleasant, and hearty nice-lady lesbian detectives to come to my aid. No, doll-girl-ghost detectives have to solve their own deaths now.

Was it Santa?

Was it capitalism?

Was it patriarchy?

Was it the Beauty Myth, always red-handed and ready for another victim? Oh, Beauty Myth, you're worse than Jack the Ripper. And like Jack the Ripper, you're getting away with murder.

Was it the Town of Boulder, eager for tourist dollars and well aware of the lure of a little human sacrifice?

I remember everything now.

When the door to my room creaks open, in a wash of blue as chilly as a white supremacist's eye, who stands there but the Blue Fairy. Under the Colorado sun, her famous indigo hair and indigo eyes have faded, sinisterly, to a watery blue. It is she the Kathy Acker™ doll has warned me against so desperately. It is she who made Little Lord Fauntleroy tell me that he could only love me if I loved myself.

She's my nemesis, the nemesis of toy children everywhere.

"Well done, JonBenet! On account of your kind heart, I forgive you all the pranks that you have played before now. Children who lovingly help their parents in their hardship and infirmity always deserve great praise and great affection, even if they cannot be cited as models of obedience and good behavior. Be sensible in the future and you will be happy."

At this point, it seems, the dream must end, and I must open my eyes and be wide awake. But I feel overcome by sleep. The Blue Fairy surely must only be a bad dream?

"Let me make you real, JonBenet," the Blue Fairy pleads, her voice phony with the unctuous concern of Boulder for Real Things, her pleading hiding the real violence of which she's always capable.

"But Stephen King said (sort of) that dead is better."

"Stephen King is a very, very good friend of mine, JonBenet, as you'll find out once you're real. He's not a character in an overblown break-up novel about Boulder that uses you as a metaphor."

What? I've been used as a metaphor? In a break-up novel about Boulder? I've been betrayed, betrayed by Kathy Acker!

It's just that moment of hesitation—what does it finally matter whether I'm a metaphor or not?—that gives the Blue Fairy her edge.

"Dead may be better, JonBenet, but real is best. You just don't know, poor child. Let me make you real. Then you'll love yourself, and then you can have Little Lord Fauntleroy again. Forever. It's the least I can do."

The Blue Fairy is as insistent as any neighborhood child molester when it comes to winning my trust for what's real. I'm terribly sleepy now—is she the Sandman, too?— and I hear her words as though underwater.

"But, Blue Fairy, to be real is to go to sleep," I yawn. "To go to sleep is to go to the place where dreams begin, the place before dreams begin. That's also where dreams end, where they die. It's the Real World. I think to be real is to be able to die, and that means to be dead, once and for all, the Second Death, Blue Fairy," I whisper, drowsily trying to edge towards the door that's still somewhat ajar.

"I'd rather be a doll, Blue Fairy..." my voice is starting to quiver. "I'm perfect like this. I don't care if I'm a toy, a... a metaphor."

The Blue Fairy leans in closely. She's stopping me from getting to the door. This close, I can smell her breath, stale with clichés and fanaticism. Her eyes are unsteady. She looks less like a fairy and more like a humdrum woman who's promoting a deranged survivalist agenda. The survival of the realest, I want to giggle, but this time, it's a giggle of panic.

"It's best to be real," snarls the Blue Fairy, exposing teeth that are a little bluish, too. Her wand glitters like a shiny new kitchen knife. She's blue like drowning, inexorable as cruelty, as motherly love. Her eyes are stainless steel. She advances, brandishing that glittering wand, inescapable as reality. Her eyes are the most watery blue, gunmetal blue, ruthlessly blue, blue as the dumb sky, the vacant, vapid, vacuous sky over Colorado, 360 sunny days a year, the sky seen through that bullet-proof Plexiglas snowglobe. Is she a fairy or a serial killer? Does it make a difference now, ever?

"YOU MUST BECOME REAL."

She backs me into a corner.

The wand pierces my heart.

And so I did, that is, I did become real.

And so I died.

For only what can die is real.

Oh, instead of this, the fiction of false endings! Fiction is always false endings: the royal messenger shows up just in time, flourishing a pardon, and you're off the gallows. Carrie reaches up from hell, from her grave, and drags you in, only you wake up, eyes agape, gasping and gawking into the camera. O and René are reunited. The carpet slinks out of Boulder, defeated. Tiffany doesn't die of Ecstasy. Little Lord Fauntleroy loves JonBenet all the more because she doesn't love herself. Why, even John and I get back together again, all is forgotten to begin anew, and this book is never written. JonBenet, moppet, adorable, precious, stays a living doll forever.

The monsters live happily ever after with their makers.

The utterance "I love you," suspended in the air like a speech bubble, neither begins nor ends anything. False endings, like false starts, can only stop in what's real, in what really happened. The ultimate cliffhanger, "I love you" would dangle you, always, over the death drop of what's real. "I love you" stays the final, never finished, fiction of a false ending and a no less false start. Reader, I married you. Without the bubble popped, without the plummet and the thud and crunch of impact, false starts and false endings would last forever. Happily ever after.

No, only what's real puts a stop to the fiction of false endings.

I die.

It's disgusting; it's real.

I'm dead.

The end.

Chapter Thirteen: JonBenet Rises

Last night I dreamed I was alive again and grown-up. In my dream, the dream of a dead doll, I woke in suffocating, clinging, invasive darkness. It took me a few moments to realize that I was buried in stamped-down dry soil, not very deep, fortunately, as I gasped and spluttered, inhaling Colorado dirt and clawing my way out.

Oh no. They'd buried me in the pet cemetery. Colorado needed its sacrificial victim, its little blonde curly-headed lamb of God so much that they had to bring me back to life. And that's where Christianity doesn't work. Only Stephen King does. So they buried me in the pet cemetery, the ancient Native American burial ground in the foothills above Boulder. That's the same place where every Christmas Boulder puts up a huge star of white electric bulbs for everyone to see this is a Christian state. Where Christmas means big light bulb stars looming over the Boulder snowglobe. Where Christmas means little murdered girls, cuter than the Lamb of God. I guess they confuse Christmas with Good Friday, the Nativity with the Resurrection.

It's Christmas Eve, the anniversary of the night they killed me.

Spitting out dirt, wiping parched soil from my eyes, I rise up. I'm tall. I'm as pale as dirty snow, and I'm rotting.

Somehow the process of resurrection took longer than Stephen King told everyone it would. That's why I'm an adult, decaying. I'm beautiful, dirty, white and pastel blue, just like the snow that's been here all winter long.

My flesh falls from my bones in long strips, long strips of Christmas garland flesh. My eyes glow, brighter than the bulbs that mark the star, clearer than the star that told the Wise Men where Baby Jesus was.

This is my Nativity. This is my Resurrection. I'm alive again and grown-up. This is my dream, damn it. I get to my feet. I'm tall. They killed me and then they couldn't live without me, so they stuck me in the old pet cemetery that used to be a Native American burial ground, where dead things come back.

Like me.

Killing me wasn't enough; they had to make sure I would come back. Why? To kill me again? Just like Little Baby Jesus on the cross of Colorado beneath the star they stick every year on the hillside? This star doesn't mark nativity, it tells people where the pet cemetery is. And it's here that even murdered dolls come back to life as grown-ups, if only in our dreams.

It's freezing cold. I'm more blue than white now, as more flesh peels off. But I'm alive again, at least for now, and grown-up.

I rise to my feet. Boulder lies beneath me, dreaming of sugarplums, sugar and spice, murdered children. They think they can kill us and bring us back to life and everything will be the same. Didn't they listen to everything Stephen King had to say? Don't they know once you come back from the pet cemetery you're a homicidal zombie? And that's just how Jesus was when he came back from his own pet cemetery.

Jesus came calling.

I've risen to my feet. I'm tall at last, no more standing on tippy-toes ever. I tower, dead eyes brighter than Nativity stars, dead flesh electric blue Christmas garlands. I rot, but beautifully. I've always done everything beautifully.

I look down on Boulder, asleep in its cozy tangle of parking lots and mini-malls, hugging itself in the arms of security devices and neighborhood watches, its walls of no-expansion policy, its zero growth. They're not safe. They'll never be safe again.

I've expanded. I've grown. I'm bigger than Boulder, grown-up at last.

If only you could see the view from here. I shiver, asleep, dead and alive again, grown-up if only in my dream.

I'll smash that snowglobe to slow-motion smithereens. Fuck Rosebud. I'm the resurrected JonBenet and I've come to take my revenge on the town that made me, that dreamt me, that killed me. Boulder—comfy clutch of the white middle class that thought it could expiate its collective guilt by sticking me in Stephen King's pet cemetery.

I throw my head back to laugh, a most ungirlish laugh, a decidedly unladylike laugh. I still have a sense of humor but I don't have a pulse; I don't need one.

I see their little Christmas lights glowing and Boulder has never looked so much like toytown before. Snow Village. More landfill Americana for the twenty-first century. And they were hoping to keep me confined to the twentieth.

You can't keep a good doll down. Or dead.

I'll be making my descent in a few minutes. And oh, the ripping and the shrieking, the tearing and the bleeding that will follow. I'll level this town with everyone in it.

Looking down on Boulder, I say to the town, like Rastignac in *Père Goriot* (it's Kathy Acker interfering again): "It's between us now." Only I'm not Rastignac and this surely isn't Paris.

I laugh again, a full-throated corpse laugh.

A few more minutes of looking down at Boulder, and then, resurrected, I descend.

ACKNOWLEDGEMENTS

No book can be written in isolation from other books, as any book attests, but this book would never have been published had it not been for the long-term support of the following friends and readers: Kathleen Chapman, as ever, Patrick Greaney, without whose continued efforts this work would never have seen the light of day and to whom I owe a great debt, Elizabeth Sheffield, who was prepared to endorse a risky text by an unknown writer, Jeffrey DeShell for his kind-hearted and witty encouragement, and Mary Burger, who provided me with invaluable editing advice and who took an early interest in publishing this book. My thanks, too, to Rikki Ducornet for commenting favorably on the first version of this, and to Peggy Kamuf for her inventive and generous introduction. My deepest thanks to everyone at Les Figues Press, this remarkable oasis in a desert of boredom, especially Teresa Carmody, who is everything one might wish for in an editor (as well as a friend and writer), and Vanessa Place, to whose pellucid vision and intellect we are all deeply indebted.

My thanks, also, to &NOW, for publishing a section of Chapter Four in *The & Now Awards: The Best Innovative Writing*, edited by Robert Archambeau, Davis Schneiderman, and Steve Tomasula (Lake Forest College, IL: &NOW Press, 2009), 127-128.

Lastly, my deep gratitude to Priya Jha and John Kehlen without whom this book would never have been written.

MICHAEL DU PLESSIS teaches Comparative Literature and English at the University of Southern California, where he is also completing a masters degree in Professional Writing. *The Memoirs of JonBenet by Kathy Acker* is his first novel. He has written about a wide variety of subjects, from Goth culture to the French *fin-de-siècle* and has also performed, amongst other venues, at Highways and at the MAK Center/ Schindler House.

PEGGY KAMUF writes on deconstructive literary theory. Her latest book is *To Follow: The Wake of Jacques Derrida*. She teaches French and comparative literature at the University of Southern California.

KLAUS KILLISCH studied painting at the Art Academy in East-Berlin from 1981-1986. His work has been represented in many exhibitions including the Biennale in Venice, Sezon Museum of Art in Tokyo, Folkwang Museum in Essen, New National Gallery in Berlin, Museum of Contemporary Art Frankfurt / Oder. Killisch lives in Berlin. <http://www.magnetberg.de>

TrenchArt : Surplus Series

Surplus series visual art
KLAUS KILLISCH

Post Office Box 7736
Los Angeles, CA 90007
www.lesfigues.com